I0671388

The Book of
Ayesha

Rated-M Wrote It

First Edition published by BookHeavy 2024

Copyright © 2024 by Rated-M Wrote It

All rights reserved. No part of this publication may be reproduced, stored or transmitted in any form or by any means, electronic, mechanical, photocopying, recording, scanning, or otherwise without written permission from the publisher. It is illegal to copy this book, post it to a website, or distribute it by any other means without permission.

This novel is entirely a work of fiction. The names, characters and incidents portrayed in it are the work of the author's imagination. Any resemblance to actual persons, living or dead, events or localities is entirely coincidental.

Rated-M Wrote It asserts the moral right to be identified as the author of this work.

Trigger Warning: This book contains explicit depictions of domestic and sexual abuse. Reader discretion is advised, and individuals sensitive to these themes are urged to exercise caution before proceeding.

First Edition

979-8-99112-690-8

In my city, the rivers flow, and Detroit stands as a spirit to show. In the heart of the struggle, a story untold unfolds, a tale of resilience fierce and bold. Burning bright like the auto's flame, Detroit's spirit, no one can tame. From Motown melodies to streets so tough, the city is known as a diamond in the rough. On concrete landscapes where dreams are sown, my city rises, not alone. From assembly lines to the music halls, Detroit's rhythm echoes through its walls. Steel-strong souls, like the Ren Cen's height, face challenges and embrace the fight. Through winters cold and summers hot, Detroit weaves a tale that can't be forgot. Cruising through the city with that smooth flow, windows down, greeting friends like, "What up doe?" In the heart of the city where legends rise, Cartier glasses rest on Detroit's wise. Through resilience and grace, they are steadfast, a symbol of triumph in Cartier glass. In my city, where the engines roar, Belle Isle whispers tales from the shore. From 7

Mile to Joy Road's embrace, in the heart of Motown, with style and grace. East Warren to Mack, the streets unfold, a narrative of stories, both young and old. Linwood and Dexter, voices of the street, a symphony of life where rhythms meet. Woodward Avenue, where dreams ignite, the hair and fashion capital shining so bright. In minks, Pelle Pelle coats, and Gator shoes, in my city, the swag's a win, never to lose. Better Made Potato Chips, a crispy delight, ice-cold Faygo bubbling, colors so bright. Chili cheese fries, Coney dogs in the air, Detroit-style pizza, a culinary affair. Anita Baker, a voice divine, Aretha Franklin, in glamour, she'd shine. Marvin Gaye's soulful serenade, Stevie Wonder's melodies will never fade. The Temptations' moves will make you get up out of your seat, Smokey Robinson's enduring rhythm never misses a beat. In the soulful echoes of Detroit's song, legends continue to rise, where they belong.

Follow me on Facebook @ ratedmwroteit

Follow me on TikTok @ iamratedm

Follow me on Instagram @ ratedmwroteit

Cover designed by @ MADALKO media

Acknowledgment

I want to express my deepest gratitude to all my supporters – your encouragement, inspiration, and belief in me have been the driving force behind this whole project. First and foremost, I want to thank God for blessing me with the ability to write; this book wouldn't exist without that. I want to give a huge thanks to my family, especially my beloved children. You're my guiding light in this creative journey, and your constant motivation keeps me going. I want to give a shout-out to my husband, who has been my rock and a constant source of love and encouragement. Your unwavering support during late nights of writing means the world to me, and I'm forever grateful for standing by me through thick and thin. To my friends, you're more than just companions; you're my cheerleaders and motivators. Your words of encouragement and shared experiences have been a much-needed break from the writing challenges, reminding me that life is all about finding that balance.

Table of contents

To: _____

Thank you for your incredible support and for accompanying me on my writing journey. Your encouragement means more to me than words can express and holds a value beyond measure. Your belief in me fuels my passion and perseverance, and for that, I am deeply grateful. I hope you find joy and connection in reading "The Book of Ayesha." Please feel free to share your thoughts and help spread the word.

Love,

_____

Date: _____

To the queen who raised me, my mom - gone but never forgotten. This one's for her and all the strong moms, amazing daughters, and fierce sisters out there. You're the heartbeat of our stories, the strength in our struggles, and the love that keeps us going. This book is dedicated to the power and beauty of women everywhere. You inspire me, and this is for you.

CHAPTER 1

Bad Vibes

Simone moaned in ecstasy, "Oh, shit! Fuck!"

In the middle of the night, my clock showed 3:29 a.m. I was awakened by the sounds of loud moaning, squeaking bed springs, and skin slapping. I knew what was going on between my mother and her boyfriend in her bedroom. I got up to go pee. Simone's door was cracked, and I saw her getting pounded from the back. I wanted to fucking vomit. I shared a room with my two sisters, Imani and Aaliyah. Imani and I shared a bunk bed, and Aaliyah slept in her twin-sized bed. My little brother, Elijah, was the only boy, so lucky for him, he had his own room. I couldn't understand how any of my siblings could sleep through those loud and disgusting noises. I was so irritated because I felt like my mother didn't give a fuck that there were children in the house, and she wasn't trying to be discreet whatsoever. Thank God it was Saturday, and I didn't have school.

I woke up some hours later, and Simone was in the kitchen cooking breakfast, wearing shorts with writing across the back, a matching tank top, and a silk headscarf over her weave. Once Dame came out of her bedroom wearing nothing but his drawers, walked into the kitchen, and gave her a loud smack on her ass, I decided not to go into the kitchen and back into my room. Damien, aka Dame, was Simone's drug-dealing boyfriend. I didn't like him, I didn't trust him, and I felt uncomfortable around him. My siblings liked him because he would give them whatever they wanted, whether it was money for the ice cream truck, toys and games for Elijah and Aaliyah, or money for Imani so that she could spend it at the beauty supply store. Simone was head-over-heels for him because he was always keeping money in her pocket, paying her bills, buying her designer clothes and purses, and dicking her down.

Simone didn't make the best choices when it came to men. My dad was a deadbeat, Imani's dad got killed in the drug game, and the relationship between Elijah and Aaliyah's dad didn't work out. Simone met Eric at a bar one night, and the two started dating not long after that. Eric and Simone were total opposites. Eric had a good job working for the U.S. Postal Service, didn't smoke, didn't drink, and was pretty laid-back. After a few months of dating, Simone ended up pregnant with Elijah. Two years later, Simone had Aaliyah with Eric. I was so mad when Eric moved out. Simone loved hood niggas and bad boys, and Eric didn't fit the description of any of that. Eric was the ideal dad I never had. He hardly raised his voice at us, but education was a priority in the household. Eric always encouraged us to get good grades and go to college, but he also had a fun side, and we would spend our summers going to Cedar Point, Belle Isle, carnivals, water parks, and the drive-in theater. The 4th of July was one of my favorite holidays as a kid because Eric would buy a shit-ton of fireworks and have the whole block of Euclid lit up. He would take us trick-or-treating on Halloween and lavish us with gifts on Christmas. I felt like we were one of those families on television when he lived with us. Simone and Eric had been broken up for two years. Looking back, I believe Eric loved my mother but was more in love with her looks.

Simone was gorgeous. She had smooth chocolate skin, a small waist, and a beautiful body that showed off her natural curves. Simone was strapped with an ass that you couldn't help but notice. Men were crazy about Simone, and when she wore sundresses, they honked their horns and begged for her number. Even after having four kids, she was still a dime. In her high school years, the boys were crazy about her. She was very popular at Northwestern High School, where she met Tony. The two started messing around in high school, and Simone became pregnant with me. I was born on April 5, 1989. Simone was seventeen when she had me. She was nineteen when she gave birth to Imani two years later. Simone didn't work and received government assistance. We were the freshest kids in the hood on welfare. Simone made money by doing hair at our house. She turned our dining room area into a beauty shop, and it always smelled like oil sheen, spritz, braid spray, hair grease, and fried hair from pressing combs, curling irons, and flat irons. If you wanted a French roll, updo, pixie cut, quick weave, a nice press-n-curl, or a sew-in, Simone was your girl, but her expertise was braiding.

We stayed in a two-family duplex on Euclid off 14th Street in Detroit that my great-aunt owned. We called her Auntie Angie. She stayed in the bottom duplex, and we stayed in the top. Auntie Angie was an older widow in her sixties, a retired nurse, had no kids, and lived alone in the bottom duplex. She had a heart of gold but took no shit from anyone. She was feisty and would tell it like it was, regardless of how anybody felt, and she loved watching *Judge Mathis*. My siblings watched cartoons in the living room while Simone made plates for breakfast. I decided to wash up, put on some clothes, and go to the bottom duplex to see Auntie Angie. I felt like I could talk to her about anything. I knocked on her door.

"Who is it?"

"Auntie, it's me."

"Come in," Auntie Angie said.

"What are you cooking?" I asked as I walked in, admiring the delicious aroma.

"Salmon croquettes, grits, potatoes, and onions," she replied.

"I want some," I said.

"I knew you would; that's why I made enough. Did Simone cook?"

"She did, but Dame is upstairs, and you know I don't like him."

"I don't blame you. I don't even want that fool in this house. I'm not a damn fool. I know what he does for a living. He's nothing but trouble. That's why his name is Damien because he's the damn devil," she said as she shook her head. "She didn't even let the sheets dry before Eric left. That damn Simone is trifling," she continued.

"She is," I said.

"Don't talk about her like that. That woman gave birth to you," Auntie Angie scolded me.

"But you said it."

"I'm grown, and that's my niece. That's still your mother, and you know what the Bible says about honoring thy mother and father. She might make some bad choices, but she feeds you, she dresses you, she ain't selling you for crack, and you ain't getting raped in a foster home. You don't have it that bad, Ayesha. I'll try to talk some sense into her."

"You missed breakfast," Simone said as she sat on the couch, smoking a blunt.

"I ate downstairs," I said.

"I know Angie was talking shit about me," Simone said.

"She was talking about Dame, and I'm glad he's finally gone," I replied.

"Dame ain't been nothing but good to y'all. You should be grateful," Simone replied.

"Because he tosses his dope money around, I should be grateful?"

"You don't say shit about that dope money when you need fresh-ass clothes for school," Simone said.

I just rolled my eyes.

"Roll your mothafucking eyes at me again!"

"Ma, how long will it be before he goes to jail or gets killed?" I replied.

"Girl, Angie is just jealous, and she's a crazy, bitter, lonely, old-ass lady," Simone said.

"That's not true," I replied.

"You know what? I'm done talking. Get the fuck outta my face, Ayesha," Simone said.

Later that evening, I overheard Simone and Auntie Angie talking.

"Simone, I need you to do my hair for church tomorrow."

"Okay, Auntie. Sit in the chair. Let's get you washed."

"Damien is no good," Auntie Angie said.

"You say that about every guy. The only guy you liked was Eric," Simone said as she rubbed her fingers through Auntie Angie's gray hair, scratching her scalp.

"Eric was a good man."

"Eric wasn't perfect, Auntie. Damien is a good man."

"Child, please. You two wouldn't be fighting all the time. A good man doesn't sell drugs to his people and poison his community. I don't trust that boy. I see the way he looks at Ayesha."

"What are you talking about? My man ain't no pedophile."

"I still don't trust him. You have a house full of girls, Simone. You can't bring any and every man around girls; hell, you can't trust too many men around little boys either."

"It's funny how you always talk about Dame, but where was that same energy for Uncle James? He almost ran you into the ground with his gambling addiction and habitual cheating ways. You almost lost this house because of him, and it was my daddy's hard-earned money that helped you keep it. I know about his other family. Uncle James had two kids with his younger mistress, and you still stayed married to him until he died. That man made you miserable. Let's not forget what he did to me," Simone said.

"You shut your mouth, or else I will slap you silly," Auntie Angie threatened.

"I'm just saying, Auntie, no disrespect."

"Damien is a wolf in sheep's clothing. That boy will cause you pain and sorrow if you keep on fooling around with him. I have a terrible feeling about this. I keep having this dream of seeing you covered in blood," Auntie Angie warned Simone.

"Auntie, stop being so superstitious," Simone said.

"I see the devil got you in the headlock," Auntie Angie replied.

"I need a favor," Simone said.

"Child, what is it now?"

"My car is still in the shop, and I need to go to the FIA office on Monday."

"Have Damien take you," Auntie Angie replied.

"Auntie, come on. I always do your hair for free."

"That's the least you can do. Considering what I charge you for rent, you're practically living here for free, Simone."

"If you want your rent money, then let me borrow your car so these people won't cut off my cash, food, and Medicaid benefits. I'll buy you a bag of jumbo shrimp and a pack of Pepsi with my Bridge Card."

"Alright, but while you're at it, add in a bag of Salt and Vinegar Better Made Potato Chips," Auntie Angie replied.

"You got it, Auntie. Thanks."

After listening to their conversation about Dame, I knew I wasn't wrong about him. I had bad vibes since the day I met him.

CHAPTER 2

Butterflies

I attended Central High School. I had just turned fifteen and was in my freshman year. I wanted to attend Northwestern High School, but my best friend had decided to go to Central, so I tagged along. My best friend and I attended Thirkell Elementary and Hutchins Middle School together, and we refused to leave each other's side in high school. Kierra had been my best friend and ride-or-die since the second grade. If I had a problem with someone, Kierra had a problem with them as well. She always had my back, and I had hers. Kierra lived within walking distance from me on Pingree Street. She was dark-skinned and had the face of a model and the hourglass shape of a grown woman. Auntie Angie used to say, *"Kierra got them child-bearing hip*s." The boys crowned Kierra for having the best body. Kierra always wanted me to do her hair, and she would always ask, *"Did you bring your flat iron to school?"* Kierra wouldn't let anyone touch her hair but me. The boys at school and around the neighborhood used to flirt with us, but I wasn't interested in many of them because they were immature, and most only wanted one thing. I was caramel, slim, and always had slanted eyes. I had shoulder-length hair that I did myself. I was so good at doing my hair that many people thought I went to the shop to get it done, and they wanted me to do their hair. I was a pro at flat-ironing, pressing, curling, and wrapping hair. I could even do 3D twisties and weave ponytails. In between classes, I would do students' hair in the girls' restroom at school. My plan after graduating high school was to get my license in cosmetology. I had plans to open a hair salon, do what I love, and be my own boss.

It was Monday morning, and I was at my locker on my way to my first-hour class, rocking a hot pink Baby Phat shirt, matching blue jeans with a hot pink Baby Phat logo on them, and white Nike Air Force Ones, when Kierra walked up behind me.

"Bitch, I got something to tell you!"

"What is it?" I replied.

She said, "Well, you look cute in your new outfit and shoes. When did you get this?"

"It was a birthday gift," I replied.

"It's cute, but back to what I was saying. Girl, guess what? TJ ate me out," Kierra said.

"What? Are you serious?"

"It felt good, and I returned the favor."

"You gave him some head, Kierra?"

"Uh, yeah," Kierra replied.

"Ugh! Kierra, that's nasty!"

"Okay, VIRGIN MARY! It's April; we have two more months until school is out, and you haven't hooked up with anybody. It's too many fine-ass niggas up in here," Kierra said.

"These niggas ain't shit. I don't plan on losing my virginity to nobody at this school."

Kierra asked, "What about Malik Davis?"

"Malik ain't interested in me," I said.

"That ain't what he told me and TJ on Saturday. You know Malik is TJ's cousin. He wanna hook up with you," Kierra replied.

"Stop fucking lying."

"I swear on my dead daddy's grave. We'll skip school this Friday at TJ's house. Malik will be there. It'll be fun, and we won't get caught," Kierra said.

"I don't know about this. I've never skipped before," I replied.

"You already get good grades. One day of missing school won't hurt you. Come on!"

"Since Malik will be there, I'll do it," I chuckled.

"Yes! Don't flake on me," Kierra replied.

Kierra's boyfriend, Terrell, aka TJ, was a freshman at Central High School. The two had met at Central and had been together for a few months. Malik was TJ's cousin, and the thought of Malik wanting to talk to me gave me butterflies. Malik was a sophomore at Central. He was tall, had this smooth, milk chocolate skin tone, always dressed fresh, smelled good, kept his hair cut, and his hair was full of waves. I had the biggest crush on him, I swear. Being on the basketball team made him a hotshot, and it seemed like every girl at Central wanted him. I'd never ditched school before, but I was willing to do it to hang out with Malik. Simone wouldn't dare let me go to a boy's house at fifteen, and I shared a room with two other girls and had no privacy, so there was no way that he could come to my house. It was lunchtime, and I was on my way to the cafeteria when Malik walked up to me with that beautiful smile on his face, brushing his waves, wearing a white tee, Girbaud jeans, and Air Jordans.

"What up doe?" Malik said.

"Hey," I replied.

"I heard you'll be at TJ's crib this Friday," Malik said.

"Damn, Kierra wasted no time telling you, huh?"

"I mean, it was her idea," Malik chuckled.

"I'll be there."

"Cool. I'm looking forward to seeing your sexy ass," Malik replied.

I almost fainted, felt butterflies in my stomach, and blushed so hard that my face turned red. I couldn't wait until Friday!

Friday had finally come, and I decided to wear this cute red polo mini dress that I bought from Rainbow. I wore my hair down with a part in the middle, applied some lip gloss that had a hint of glitter in it, and put on my favorite cucumber melon body spray. The dress I wore had buttons on it, and I opened the first two buttons to show off a bit of cleavage. I was feeling cute and nervous at the same time. After hearing the first-hour bell, Kierra and I left school and walked to TJ's. TJ stayed in the Russell Woods Apartments, which were within walking distance of the school.

TJ answered the door and said, "What up?"

"Hey," I said.

"Damn, you look good," Malik said to me as he sat on the loveseat.

"Thank you," I replied.

Kierra said to TJ, "Nigga, your mama will fucking kill you if she smells weed in her house! Put that shit out!"

"Kierra, chill. My mama won't be home until after six. The smell will be gone by then. Hit this shit," TJ said to Kierra as he passed her the blunt. "You smoke?" TJ asked.

"No. If I came home high, my mom would nut up," I replied. "Malik, do you smoke?" I asked.

"This lame-ass nigga don't smoke," TJ replied to me.

"Nigga, she was talking to me," Malik replied. "I don't fuck with that shit. I'm not trying to get kicked off the basketball team, and I heard that weed destroys brain cells. Look at TJ. I would hate to end up like him," Malik joked.

TJ laughed, "Fuck you, you bitch-ass nigga!"

"I ain't the one in LD classes," Malik replied.

"Them mothafucking teachers don't know shit. I don't have a learning disability," TJ replied.

"This nigga is supposed to be in the tenth grade with me," Malik said.

"I can't help it if I flunked the third grade. Third grade was hard as fuck," TJ said.

"Since when did you start smoking?" I asked Kierra.

"Girl, fucking with this nigga," Kierra said as she hit the blunt and pointed at TJ.

"Yo, I saw Ayesha's mama at school one day, and her mama is thick as fuck," TJ said.

Kierra socked TJ in the arm and said, "Really?"

"Ouch! You mad? I'll make it up to you," TJ said as he led Kierra into his room and closed the door.

"Why you way over there? Come sit next to me," Malik said.

I sat next to Malik, feeling nervous and shy.

"You stay near Linwood by Kierra?"

"Yeah. How do you know?"

"Kierra told me. Plus, I hoop at the Joseph Walker Williams Center sometimes. I might need to come see you one day," Malik smiled.

"Where do you stay?"

"I'm a Dexter nigga, baby. I stay on Glendale."

"Oh, that's not far."

"Not far at all. That's why you should come through," Malik smirked.

Malik had me blushing so hard.

"I heard about your sixteenth birthday party. I'm sorry that I couldn't make it. Kierra told me that it was nice," I said.

"I wanted to see you there. You hurt a nigga's feelings," Malik joked.

"I had to babysit that night. I'm the oldest of four. It's hard for me to get out sometimes because I'm always babysitting," I said.

"Straight?"

"Yeah. I have a twelve-year-old sister, an eight-year-old brother, and a six-year-old sister," I replied.

"Damn, it must be tough being the oldest. I'm the youngest," Malik said.

"Are your parents still together?" I asked.

"Yeah. They've been married for over twenty years," Malik replied.

"Malik, you're lucky to have both parents in the same household. I only see my dad every blue moon."

"I'm sorry to hear that," Malik replied. "Let's change the subject. Real talk, I heard you got a crush on me," he said.

"Maybe I do."

"I knew it. Most girls can't resist a nigga like me," Malik joked.

"Boy, stop," I replied.

"All jokes aside, I like you a lot, and I couldn't wait for us to be alone together," Malik said.

At that moment, we shared a kiss. One peck turned into more passionate kissing on the lips, and then Malik stuck his tongue in my mouth, and we were tongue-kissing. At that moment, I felt a tingling feeling. I had never kissed a boy this way. My hormones were raging. I see why Auntie Angie said that kissing leads to pregnancy.

We hung out at TJ's house until school dismissed. On the bus ride home, I couldn't stop thinking about Malik. My mind kept replaying the kiss we shared, and I couldn't wait to see him again.

"You in trouble," Imani said as she stood on the porch with her hand on her hip.

"Shut up," I said as I walked up the stairs to our duplex.

Simone sat on the sofa, smoking a Black & Mild, and asked, "How was school?"

"I took a test today," I replied.

"For which class?" Simone asked.

"English."

"Cut the bullshit, Ayesha. The school called. I already know you skipped school."

"Ooh," Imani teased me.

Simone yelled at Imani, "Shut the fuck up, Imani!" Then she said to me, "You might as well tell me the fucking truth."

"Truth is, I was with Kierra."

"With Kierra, where?"

"I was at Kierra's boyfriend's house," I replied.

"Why the fuck do you smell like weed?"

"Kierra's boyfriend was smoking, but I swear, I didn't smoke."

"I knew you had to be with Kierra's fast ass. I bet she was sucking and fucking. Since you wanna be a fucking follower, I'm putting you on punishment for two weeks."

"Ma!"

"Shut the fuck up! I'm being nice by giving you two weeks! I should put you on punishment for a month," Simone yelled.

When I arrived at school the following Monday, Ms. Hill approached me in the hallway and said, "Miss Jones, I need to speak with you. I saw you with Miss Johnson on Friday. You skipped your classes. That's very unlike you, Miss Jones. You're a good student. I know Miss Johnson is your homegirl, but don't let her get you in trouble. Don't let it happen again. Have a wonderful day."

Ms. Hill was my student counselor. I liked her a lot. She was very down-to-earth and straightforward. I felt bad for disappointing her, but I didn't regret my time with Malik.

CHAPTER 3

Virginity

After I got off punishment, I spent time with Malik. Malik told me that he and I were together. He never showed me much affection when we were at school, and he wanted to be low-key about our relationship. When I asked him why he wanted to keep our relationship such a secret, he said he didn't want people in our business and being messy. That was understandable in my mind. Kierra and I were preparing to leave my house to meet Malik and TJ at the park.

"You ready?" Kierra asked.

"Yeah, let's bounce," I replied.

Simone walked into the living room and asked, "Where y'all going?"

"To the park," I said.

"Take Elijah and Aaliyah with you," Simone replied.

"Why?"

"I'm getting ready to take a nap, that's why," Simone said.

"Do I have to?"

"Ayesha, you don't have a choice."

"Come on," I said to Elijah and Aaliyah, feeling annoyed.

After we arrived at the park, Kierra, TJ, Malik, and I sat on the bench. Kierra pointed at a girl named Talisha.

"Look at the crack baby over there," Kierra said.

"That's mean, Kierra," I replied.

"I don't give a fuck! Fuck her! She ain't nothing but a busto," Kierra said.

"How do you know?" I asked.

"Zayvion told me that he, Tez, Peanut, and Cory ran a train on her. I know he ain't lying because Zayvion stays down the street from me, and I saw Talisha coming out of Zayvion's house after it happened," Kierra said.

"That's nasty. Talisha should have more respect for herself," I replied.

"The crack baby is cute," TJ said.

"Nigga, please. I look better than her. You know Zayvion paid Tiny five dollars to suck his dick. Like mother, like daughter," Kierra said.

"Zayvion is fifteen, and Tiny is a grown-ass woman," I replied.

"I guess age ain't nothing but a number. Shit, crackheads will do anything to buy a rock," TJ said.

"I dare you to ask Talisha for some head," Kierra said to TJ.

"Okay, bet," TJ replied. "Talisha! Can I get some head?" TJ yelled while Talisha sat on the swing.

The four of us laughed when Talisha gave us the middle finger before she left the park. Talisha Thompson was a girl in the neighborhood who stayed on Delaware Street, across from the park we were at. She attended Northwestern High School and was the same age as me, and her mother was on drugs. Talisha was caramel like me and one of the neighborhood's prettiest girls. She lived with her big sister, Dawn. Dawn was in her twenties, drop-dead gorgeous, and looked like she could star in a music video or movie. She worked as an exotic dancer and was the cool big sister who would talk to us about boys and sex. *"Don't give these broke-ass niggas no pussy,"* Dawn would always say to us. Simone and Auntie Angie stopped me from hanging with Talisha. Auntie Angie thought Talisha was fast, too grown, and a bad influence on me because of how she dressed, and she thought that Dawn was a bad role model. Simone didn't want me hanging with Talisha because of her beef with Dawn. Word around the hood was that Dawn messed around with Dame. Knowing Dame, that was probably true. Dawn and Talisha were daughters of the neighborhood crackhead, which was a woman nicknamed Tiny. Charlene Thompson, aka Tiny, had been strung out on crack for years, leaving Dawn to raise Talisha. I remember when Tiny tried to sell Simone some of Talisha's toys to buy crack when we were younger.

"Let's go over by the shed and leave these two lovebirds alone," TJ said to Kierra before smacking Kierra on her ass.

"I have something to tell you. I love you, Ayesha," Malik said as I sat on his lap on the park bench.

"I love you, too," I replied like a naïve teenage girl would.

We had been together for a few weeks, and I believed anything Malik told me. We kissed, and then Malik said, "Maybe we can do more than just kissing one day."

"What do you mean?"

"You know what I mean. I'm ready to take our relationship to the next level. I'll have the crib to myself next Saturday. I want you to slide through," Malik replied.

I heard Aaliyah crying and quickly ran over to the swings. Elijah stood up while swinging when Aaliyah tried to copy and fell off the swings.

"Are you okay, Leelee?" I asked.

Aaliyah cried and replied, "I wanna go home!"

"I told her not to stand on the swings," Elijah said.

"If she sees you standing on the swings, she'll do the same, Elijah," I replied. "Malik, I have to get my little brother and sister home," I said.

Kierra asked me, "Why are you leaving, and why is Aaliyah crying?"

"She fell and hurt herself, but she's fine. I have to get her home. That's why I didn't want them to come."

"Come to my house after you take them home," Kierra said.

Dawn came out of nowhere and asked, "One of y'all got a problem with my sister?"

"I don't," TJ replied.

"Y'all had a lot of mouth. Why y'all quiet now? I'ma warn y'all one time. If you fuck with my sister again, I will fuck y'all up. I fight kids," Dawn threatened before walking away.

"Talisha's sister is fine as fuck," TJ said.

"Fuck you and that bitch," Kierra told TJ.

"You didn't have all that mouth a few seconds ago," TJ said.

"You didn't say shit either," Kierra replied.

"I don't hit women," TJ replied.

"I'll see you in a bit," I told Kierra.

When I arrived home, Aaliyah whined, and Simone asked, "What's wrong with my baby?"

"She fell off the swings at the park," I said.

"How the fuck did she do that?"

"She was standing up on the swings."

"And you let her do that shit?" Simone questioned.

"I didn't know," I replied.

"You were supposed to be watching them. Where were you when this happened?" Simone questioned.

"She was kissing her boyfriend," Elijah said.

"Shut up, Elijah!" I yelled.

"Boyfriend? What boyfriend?" Simone asked.

"I have a boyfriend named Malik."

"Aaliyah hurt herself because you weren't watching her. This shit wouldn't have happened if you weren't so busy up in some nigga's face!"

"She didn't hurt herself that bad."

"That's not the fucking point, Ayesha! What if I had to take her to the hospital, and she ended up with a concussion? You are starting to piss me the fuck off. First, you skipped school, and now this. Do I need to take you down to the clinic and get you on birth control?"

"Ma, all we did was kiss."

"Kissing will turn into fucking! You think I don't know? I was seventeen when I had you."

"I won't end up pregnant. I'm not like you."

"You say that shit now because you think you're so smart and get good grades. You're more like me than you think. Look here. I thought the same thing, and look at what happened. I was getting good grades when I ended up pregnant with you, Miss Smarty Pants."

"Oh my God, you haven't even met Malik."

"I don't have to meet him to know that he wants some pussy. I keep track of your periods. You better not miss a period. I'm not fucking playing with you, Ayesha."

After Simone chewed me out, I went to Kierra's house. We chilled in Kierra's bedroom, listening to FM 98 WJLB. Her house was my getaway spot.

"I'm losing my virginity to Malik."

"Shit, I don't blame you. He can get it," Kierra replied.

"Malik's mom will be working late, and his dad will be on a business trip next weekend, so we'll have the house to ourselves. You and TJ have to come with me. We'll say that we're going to Northland and tell my mom that I'm spending the night with you. I really like Malik. I'm serious about him being my first. I refuse to get pregnant and end up as a teenage mother like my mom did," I said.

"You won't get pregnant. Just use a condom. And if Malik doesn't have a condom, he can pull out. That's what TJ does sometimes."

"I'm not taking that chance, Kierra."

"What if he wants some head?" Kierra asked.

"Ugh! Sucking dick is nasty. I don't see how girls can do that," I replied.

"It's not nasty. If you don't do it, another girl will. That's how bitches be getting cheated on."

"I remember when you lost your virginity."

"Girl, I was in the eighth grade at Hutchins. I skipped school with Tez and let him pop my cherry in his basement," Kierra replied.

Kierra's mother, Renee, walked into the room and said, "Ayesha, Simone just called. You gotta go home and watch the kids. Tell her I'll pay her to do my hair next weekend."

"But I just got here."

"And it's time for you to go. You better listen to your mama," Renee replied. "Kierra, why is my sink full of fucking dishes? All you do is eat, sleep, shit, and run around with that nigga! I don't need any grandkids! As soon as you turn eighteen, find somewhere else to live! Lazy black bitch!" Renee yelled.

Renee would get drunk often and unleash her drunken anger on Kierra. Renee would verbally abuse Kierra by calling her names, cursing her out, and belittling her. She used to attack Kierra physically, but once Kierra got old and big enough and fought Renee back, she stopped putting her hands on Kierra. Kierra used to cry when Renee would go into a drunken rage, but now it seemed like she was used to it.

"I'm so tired of that drunk-ass bitch. I fucking hate her. She doesn't treat my brother like this. I'm moving out when I turn seventeen. TJ will be eighteen by then, and we plan to get an apartment."

"You know how she gets when she starts drinking. I'm so mad right now. Why can't Imani babysit? She'll be thirteen next month. I was younger than her when I would watch them."

"Girl, both of our mamas are on some bullshit right now, but I'll come over as soon as I'm done with these dishes. I'm not in the mood to deal with my drunk-ass mama tonight," Kierra said.

"Okay, cool," I replied.

When I arrived home, Dame was smoking a blunt on the porch and said, "Pretty girls like you shouldn't be looking so mean."

"I wouldn't look so mean if I didn't have to watch my mama's kids," I replied.

"Maybe this will make you feel better. Here you go," Dame said as he handed me a fifty-dollar bill. "Yo, where Kierra at?"

"Why the fuck is he asking about a fifteen-year-old girl? Fucking creepy-ass nigga," I thought to myself.

"I thought that girl was older than fifteen, with her pretty chocolate self. Ooh-wee, I know these young niggas be on her head. I see you got a boyfriend. I saw you hugged-up with him at the park. That nigga can hoop his ass off. Did you let him hit it yet? You can tell me, I won't tell Simone," Dame said. "Hey, Miss Angie. You need help with carrying those bags?" Dame asked Auntie Angie.

Auntie Angie had pulled up just in time with groceries in the trunk of her Ford Taurus and said, "I'm doing fine. I'm blessed and highly favored. Ayesha can help me with the groceries," Auntie Angie replied to Dame.

"Auntie, do you need anything? I can reimburse you for the food you bought. I know it's hard living on a fixed income and all," Dame said, pulling out a wad of money.

"You must think I'm Simone. Your money doesn't impress me. I know how you got that money, and it ain't from flipping burgers. People like you destroy these neighborhoods. You give out turkeys on Thanksgiving to the elderly and toys to the poor kids for Christmas, but turn around and sell that poison to their families. Only the devil would do that. Sadly, these young boys look up to you. Hmph, some role model you are. I don't need a dime from you. I'm doing just fine, and if I were you, I would leave now. Don't let my old age fool you. I will pop a cap in your ass," Auntie Angie replied.

"I'm scared of you, Miss Angie," Dame laughed as he got in his customized old-school Chevy Caprice and waited for Simone.

"If I take money from him, I might as well take money from Satan himself," Auntie Angie said to me.

When Friday came, I was leaving to meet up with Kierra. Eric arrived to pick up Elijah and Aaliyah for the weekend and said, "Ayesha, that blue jean skirt you're wearing looks a little too short. Where are you going?"

"I'm meeting up with Kierra, and we're taking the Dexter bus to Northland Mall."

"You don't have to take the bus; I'll drop you young ladies off."

"That's okay. We don't mind taking the bus," I replied.

"Are you telling me that you would rather take that long bus route to Northland instead of getting a free ride that would save you time?"

"Yeah," I replied.

"You and Kierra must be meeting some boys up there."

"Why would you say that?"

"There was a time when I was fifteen, Ayesha. Who is he?"

"His name is Malik," I replied.

"Is this Malik guy a friend or your boyfriend?"

"He's my boyfriend," I said.

"Does Simone know about this Malik character?"

"Yes," I replied.

"Ayesha, you're a very beautiful young lady. I'm not surprised that you have a boyfriend at this age, but I need you to stay focused. Boys can be a major distraction, and most of them at this age are more focused on your body than your mind. Do you remember the Seven B's that I told you about?"

"Books Before Boys Because Boys Bring Babies; I already know," I replied.

"Don't make me hurt that boy," Eric said.

"I'm sorry that I couldn't make it to your wedding, Eric."

"Ayesha, I understand. I wouldn't want you to feel like you're betraying Simone. Simone hates Tanya. Tanya and I went to high school together, and I've known her for years. Hopefully, you'll meet her one day," Eric said.

"Well, I hope everything works out," I said.

"Although Simone and I aren't together anymore, I still love and care about you. I've known you since you were five years old. Regardless of blood, genetics, or any DNA, you're my first daughter. Well, I'm not trying to hold you up. I want you and Kierra to be safe. Remember what I said, Ayesha. Bye."

CHAPTER 4

The First Time

I met up with Kierra, and we took the Dexter bus to Malik's house. Malik stayed on Glendale Avenue off Dexter. When we arrived, his house was elegantly furnished and decorated. The walls had framed artwork and pictures of him and his family. The finished basement of his home was equipped with a black leather sectional, a big-screen TV, and a pool table. Kierra and TJ stayed in the basement, and I headed upstairs with Malik.

"Don't smoke that shit in here! Smoke that shit outside," Malik said to TJ.

"Nigga, you scary as fuck. Fuck it then," TJ replied as he put the blunt away.

Malik's room was painted dark blue, and posters of some of his favorite basketball stars, such as Michael Jordan, Kobe Bryant, and Allen Iverson, were on the wall. There was also a poster of 50 Cent from the *Get Rich or Die Tryin'* album cover. Malik had played basketball since elementary school, and his dresser was filled with trophies of his basketball achievements. He had a TV in his room with cable, a stereo system, and a PlayStation 2. It was obvious that Malik was quite spoiled.

"You have a nice house, Malik."

"Thanks. My mom is a neat freak, and she decorated the crib. No one can sit in the living room, so we go to the basement. My mom is bougie as fuck. I'm surprised we don't live in Oakland County because of her," Malik chuckled. "You want something to drink? We got cans of Faygo and bottled water," Malik said.

"I'll take a Faygo."

"What flavor? We got red, orange, grape, and cola."

"I'll take a red," I replied.

We talked for about thirty minutes, and then we ended up making out. Malik was tongue-kissing me, kissing and sucking on my neck, grabbing my breasts, and putting his fingers inside my panties. "Damn, you wet," Malik whispered.

Malik walked over to his stereo system and put on a mix CD with slow jams. When he turned back around, I was in his bed, dressed in my bra and panties. Malik asked, "You sure you wanna do this?"

"I'm sure."

Jagged Edge's *What You Tryin' To Do* played in the background.

Malik took his clothes off, got on top of me, and started kissing my neck and sucking on my breasts. He took my panties off and grabbed a condom from his nightstand. The pleasure that I felt from him kissing my neck and sucking on my breasts turned into pain after he proceeded to insert his penis inside of me. I felt like my vagina was being ripped open. The pain continued for the next ten minutes. After we were done and he put on his clothes, I noticed a stain of blood on his bed sheets.

"Don't worry about that. That's what happens the first time. I'll wash that shit off," Malik said as he noticed me looking at the blood.

As we were preparing to leave, TJ said to Malik as he gave Malik a dap, "I know you had fun! I swear, virgin pussy is the best pussy."

"Shut the fuck up and walk us to the bus stop," Kierra said to TJ.

Once the bus arrived, I kissed Malik goodbye, got on the bus, and headed to Kierra's house.

"How was it? I want all the juicy details, bitch," Kierra said on the bus.

"Bitch, that shit was painful. I don't see how you can enjoy that shit. I didn't get any pleasure from it at all."

"The first time is the worst. Was Malik's dick big?"

"It was too big," I chuckled.

"Did he eat you out?"

"No, and I didn't suck his dick," I replied.

"Did he use a condom, or did he go in raw?"

"He used a condom. I'm not getting pregnant."

"You can't get pregnant on the first time."

"Kierra, what sex education class taught you that?"

"It's true," Kierra said.

"That's so far from the truth," I replied.

"You and Malik would make a pretty baby," Kierra joked.

"I'm not having anyone's baby anytime soon, Kierra."

"Oh my God," Kierra said as she looked at me with fear in her eyes.

"What? Bitch, what?"

"Malik put a hickey on you," Kierra replied.

"Are you serious? Fuck!"

"Psych!"

"Kierra, you fucking play too much."

After I lost my virginity to Malik, Malik had been distant. I would call him, and he would always tell me that he would call me back, but he never did. Malik and I didn't hang out anymore, and he hardly spoke to me at school. We had sex that once, and he didn't even press to have sex with me again. Something wasn't right. It was a typical day at school when I fucked around and found out.

I saw Malik standing at his locker, talking to a sophomore named Nicole Simmons. Nicole was pretty, light-skinned, and was on the cheerleading team with Kierra. Malik and Nicole shared a kiss, and before I could confront Malik, Kierra pulled me into the girls' restroom.

"Kierra, what the fuck are you doing? Malik got me fucked up!"

Kierra handed me a piece of paper and said, "Girl, look at this."

The piece of paper had the names of girls at Central. Next to the names of the girls were boys on the school's basketball team, and some of the girls' names were crossed out. I saw my name next to Malik's name, and it was crossed out like some of the other names.

"What's this?"

"It's called a *hit list*. It's a list of girls who the boys on the basketball team make bets on who they can have sex with. All the girls' names who are crossed out had sex with someone. I snatched it from one of the players on the team," Kierra replied.

"Are you telling me that Malik used me?"

"Yeah. I'm sorry. I shouldn't have hooked you up with him. Malik kept asking about you and acted like he really liked you. I didn't know this would happen."

"Kierra, you don't have to apologize. It's not your fault; it's his, and he won't fucking get away with this," I said as I stormed out of the restroom.

Nicole was gone, and Malik was still standing by the locker with his friends when I walked up and said, "So I was a bet to you? You used me!"

"I had a good time. We had fun, and we can do it again if you want," Malik said as he and his friends laughed at me.

I slapped him on the face, ripped up the list, threw the pieces of paper in his face, and said, "You're a piece of shit. I hate you."

"Lucky I don't hit girls," Malik said to me before I walked away.

"Malik, how could you do my best friend like that? Fuck you and the rest of you lame-ass niggas," Kierra said to Malik and his friends.

I went back into the restroom and cried, "Kierra, I feel so fucking stupid."

"Don't feel stupid. These niggas ain't shit," Kierra said as she handed me some tissue.

"He acted like I meant nothing to him and had the nerve to show out in front of his friends, and he's messing around with another girl. What does Nicole have that I don't?"

"Nicole is okay-looking, but you look better than that high-yellow bitch!"

"He lied to me and used me. I should tell Nicole what type of nigga he is," I said.

"Girl, what good would that do? All he'll do is deny it. Nicole will believe him over you, and you'll be looking like a jealous-ass bitch," Kierra replied.

"He made it seem like he really liked me, and it was just to have sex with me. I can't believe I wasted losing my virginity on him."

"Now that I think about it, I remember seeing Nicole at his birthday party. I didn't think anything of it because this was before you started talking to Malik," Kierra said.

"What should I do, Kierra?"

"Stop crying and move the fuck on. Fuck Malik! Find you a new nigga. Crying won't fix shit."

Days later, I saw Malik walking the halls with his arm around Nicole. She was wearing his hoodie. They were a couple, and Malik acted as if I never existed. I was in the restroom at school, fixing my hair and applying my lip gloss, when Nicole walked in and applied her mascara.

Nicole asked, "Can I ask you something?"

"What is it?"

"I see the way you and your friend Kierra look at me. You and Kierra look at me like you two have a problem with me or something. Is it because of Malik?"

"Malik is not the guy that you think he is. He's a liar and a user."

"I told Malik this would happen. All these hating-ass females are trying to cause trouble in our relationship. I swear, females are so messy," Nicole said.

"I'm not jealous or messy. I'm just telling you the truth."

"Malik told me that you would try to break us up. He warned me about you and said that you're obsessed with him and that you're nothing but a groupie. He said that he hit it and quit it, and you've been stalking him ever since. You're nothing but a smash and pass," Nicole said.

"He's fucking lying!"

"No, you're the fucking liar. Stay away from him," Nicole said before she exited the restroom.

CHAPTER 5

Heartbroken

I experienced my first heartbreak at the age of fifteen. Malik had broken my heart, and I wasn't taking it very well. All I did was go to school, come home, eat, and sleep. I didn't even hang out with Kierra. It was hard going to school because I would see Malik and Nicole together, and it reminded me of how he played me. I was so hurt.

Simone stormed into my room and yelled, "Ayesha! Get the fuck up!"

"What?"

"Don't say *what* to me! It's almost two o'clock! Wake your ass up! What's wrong?"

"Nothing," I replied.

"You sick? You better not be pregnant!"

"I'm not pregnant."

"If you say so. I need you to go to the store. Imani just started her first period, and she needs some pads. I need you to take my Bridge Card and get what's on this list," Simone said as she handed me her Bridge Card, a twenty-dollar bill, and a paper list.

"Ma, give me a minute."

"Ayesha, get up, go wash your ass, and go do what the fuck I said! You don't have a fucking job! Ain't no reason for you to sleep all day!"

"She gets on my fucking nerves," I mumbled to myself.

Auntie Angie sat on the porch and asked, "Ayesha, are you heading to the store?"

"Yeah."

Auntie Angie handed me a ten-dollar bill and asked, "Can you get me some shrimp fried rice from the Chinese food place?"

"Okay."

"Thank you," Auntie Angie replied.

As I walked to the grocery store on 12th Street, Zayvion rode his bike up to me. Zayvion was a boy from the neighborhood. He was brown-skinned with braids and was annoying as fuck.

"Ayesha, I heard you got that cherry popped," Zayvion said.

"Who the fuck told you that?"

"Who else? You know Kierra can't hold water. She ran her mouth to the whole hood. That's fucked up. I wanted to pop your cherry," Zayvion said.

I yelled, "Get the fuck away from me, Zayvion!"

Zayvion replied, "Fuck you then, you stuck-up-ass bitch!"

"Fuck you, you French mouse-looking-ass nigga!"

"That's why I'ma fuck your fine-ass mama one day," Zayvion said.

"My mama wouldn't fuck a broke and dusty-ass nigga like you," I replied as Zayvion rode off on his bike.

I was so pissed at Kierra for telling my business, especially to Zayvion. I decided to head to her house before going to the grocery store.

"She ain't here. I'll let her know that you came by," Renee said when she answered the door.

"Okay, thank you."

"No problem," Renee replied.

When I returned home with the items from the store, Imani was wrapped in a blanket, sitting on the couch, watching cartoons with Elijah and Aaliyah.

"Here you go," I said to Imani as I sat next to her and gave her the package of pads.

"Thanks," Imani replied.

"Are you okay?"

"No. My stomach hurts. I woke up with blood in my panties," Imani replied.

"Welcome to womanhood. I started my first period when I was twelve. It happened to me while I was at school. Thank God no one noticed," I said.

"Mama said that I could end up pregnant now and told me not to be doing anything nasty with boys," Imani said.

"She's right. Please take my advice. Boys are stupid. There will come a time when some boy might try to talk you into doing something nasty, but don't let him. All he's trying to do is use you, that's it. Remember these Seven B's. Books Before Boys Because Boys Bring Babies," I replied.

I walked into the kitchen and said, "Ma, can I ask you something?"

"I'm broke; I don't have any money," Simone replied as she prepared to make Hamburger Helper for dinner.

"I'm not asking for money," I replied.

"What is it?"

"Can I transfer to another school?"

"School is almost out in a few weeks. Why do you wanna transfer now?"

"I mean, for the upcoming school year. I can't stay at Central," I replied.

"Why?"

"It's too much drama at Central," I said.

"Child, it's drama at every damn school," Simone replied.

"Ma, please? I'll go to Northwestern, Northern, Murray-Wright, anywhere but Central."

"No, Ayesha. I'm not going through all that paperwork to transfer you to another school. You wanted to go to Central so bad, so stay there. Wait a minute. Something ain't right. What's the real reason you wanna transfer? Don't lie to me."

"It's Malik."

"What does Malik have to do with you wanting to switch schools? Why are you letting this nigga run you away? What happened?"

"He lied, used, and embarrassed me," I replied.

"Used you? Used you how? Did you give it up to him?"

I didn't respond.

"You hear me talking to you! Answer the damn question, Ayesha!"

"Yes, I lost my virginity to him. I only had sex once," I replied.

"Well, I'll be damned. Let me guess. Malik told you a bunch of sweet lies, got what he wanted, and moved on to the next girl?"

"How did you know?"

"That's how these niggas do. Things ain't much different today than when I was in high school. They tell you how much they love you, they wanna marry you, how pretty you are, but it's just a tactic to get some pussy. You fell for his bullshit and gave him something valuable that you will never get back. Do you know why I'm always on your ass?"

I asked, "Why?"

"Because I don't want you to be having babies in high school, becoming a single mother, unmarried with four kids and three baby daddies like me. I expect better from you."

"I know."

"Please tell me that he used a condom," Simone said.

"He did," I replied.

"I'm not happy about my daughter popping pussy at fifteen, but at least you made him use a condom. Always use protection, even if you are on the pill or the shot. Birth control will only protect you from getting pregnant, but it won't protect you from catching chlamydia, gonorrhea, herpes, or HIV. You don't wanna catch no STD from these dirty-dick niggas out here, especially one you can't cure. I lost my virginity when I was in the ninth grade to Terrance Cole. He was fine as hell; he looked just like El DeBarge. I was fourteen and gave it up to a high school senior. I got played, but I'm still not transferring you to another school. That's what you get for being hot-in-the-ass. I learned my lesson; you gotta learn yours."

The next day, Kierra came over to my house and said, "Bitch, long time no see."

I sat on my porch, watching Elijah and Aaliyah play outside, and said, "Why the fuck did you tell Zayvion that I lost my virginity? I don't even fuck with him."

"Chill, it ain't that serious," Kierra replied.

"It's serious to me. That shit is personal."

"Ayesha, stop tripping. It must be that time of the month."

"You told my fucking business to the whole hood, but I'm tripping? Telling Zayvion is like telling the whole hood. As my best friend, I trust you with my secrets. That's fake as fuck, Kierra."

Kierra replied, "Ever since you broke up with Malik, you've been a bitch. We barely talk or hang out, and you walk around with a funky-ass attitude all the time. I was there for you when Malik played you, but now I see why he did what he did to you! You deserve it!"

"Fuck you, Kierra!"

"Fuck you too, bitch!"

Auntie Angie came outside and said, "Ayesha Nicole Jones and Kierra Christina Johnson, have you lost your damn minds out here? I should wash both of your mouths out with soap! What the hell is going on?"

"Ayesha is mad at me," Kierra said.

Auntie Angie replied, "Well, Ayesha seems to be mad at the whole damn world lately. Ayesha, what's going on with you?"

"I said some things that I shouldn't have said," Kierra said.

Auntie Angie asked me, "Is that true?"

"Yeah," I replied.

"Well, whatever it is, apologize to each other and move on. You two have been friends since you could barely wipe your asses right. True friendship is valuable. Kierra made a mistake, Ayesha. Forgive her. If you made a mistake, I would be telling Kierra to do the same," Auntie Angie said.

"Sorry," Kierra said.

"I accept your apology, and I'm sorry for the way I've been acting lately."

Auntie Angie replied, "And if I catch you two talking like that again, I'll give both of you a Mississippi ass-whupping."

"Auntie Angie is crazy, but I missed you," Kierra said after Auntie Angie went into the house.

"I missed you, too. I'm just heartbroken. I hate that I'm going back to Central. I tried to ask my mom to transfer me to another school, and she wasn't going for it."

"Why transfer and leave me? You gave it up to a cute and popular nigga on the basketball team. You fucked him; big deal. It ain't like you're known as the school slut."

"It still hurts. Malik acts so differently with Nicole. He walks her to class, lets her wear his jackets and hoodies, holds her hands, kisses and hugs her, and lets the whole school know that they're together. He even bought her a necklace for her birthday. They're known as one of the school's cutest couples. He's so public about his relationship with her but kept me a secret."

"Malik is cute and all, but you gotta get over him. There are plenty of fish in the sea."

"You're right. It's time for me to move on. Where the hoes at?" I joked.

"Girl, the hoes are at the basketball court. Bitch, let's go," Kierra replied.

"Okay, come on."

"Can you do my hair before we go? I need a ponytail and some swoops," Kierra said as she handed me a black bag with track hair in it.

"Bitch, that's the only reason why you came over. Come on," I said as we headed into the house.

"Bitch, you know I love you," Kierra said as she put her arm around me.

CHAPTER 6

Deadbeat

It was the last day of school, and I was happy about it. No more waking up in the early mornings, no more going to class, no more assignments, exams, or homework, no more drama, and most of all, no more Malik. I would finally be free after dismissal later that afternoon. When I arrived at school, I saw Dame's car parked out front. I thought Simone would be getting out of the car, and I didn't understand why Simone would be coming up to the school unless it was to talk to my teachers. I was doing well in school, so the teachers had no reason to complain about me. Was it a family emergency? Why else would Simone be at my school? The person who got out of Dame's car wasn't Simone. It was Kierra.

I thought to myself, *"What the fuck is she doing riding with Dame?"*

"Hey," Kierra said to me.

"Hey. I saw you getting out of Dame's car. Care to explain that?"

"Girl, I was running late, and that's why I didn't catch the bus with you. Dame saw me at the bus stop and offered me a ride," Kierra replied.

"Are you sure that's all he offered you?"

"Yeah, why?"

"Just asking," I replied.

"I did smoke with him on the way to school."

"Are you fucking kidding me? A grown-ass man shouldn't be smoking with a teenage girl."

"Girl, chill the fuck out, and why you don't like Dame? He's cool as fuck."

"Fuck him. He ain't shit," I replied.

"Dame seems cool to me, and he got money," Kierra said.

"Drug money," I replied.

"And? Shit, I need me a nigga who can cash me out," Kierra said.

"Kierra, you have a boyfriend. What about TJ?"

"That broke-ass nigga can't afford to take me to the movies. I'm always paying for both of us. Girl, do you know that nigga didn't even have bus fare the last time we went? I had to pay for his bus fare and cur movie tickets!"

"The niggas who slang drugs end up in jail or dead," I replied.

"Girl, I don't give a fuck. The doughboys are the ones with money. I need a nigga with a car, who can take me out, take me shopping, and buy me name-brand shit," Kierra replied.

"Like my Auntie Angie said, people like Dame destroy people and the communities. Look at Tiny."

"Tiny had a choice, and I don't think anyone put a gun to her head and made her smoke crack. Besides, the government keeps the drugs on the streets. You might as well say that Dame is a government employee."

"Kierra, I can't deal with you."

After school was dismissed, I was looking for Kierra, but she was nowhere to be found. I decided to walk toward the bus stop and take the bus home by myself, and a male voice yelled, "Esha!"

I turned around and saw the man wearing a navy blue Dickies outfit and a matching Detroit snapback on his head, and I replied, "Daddy?"

I hadn't seen my daddy since my thirteenth birthday when he came over to the house and gave me a birthday card with a twenty-dollar bill in it. I would talk to him on the phone from time to time, but I hadn't seen him in two years. It wasn't because he lived out of state. We stayed in the same state; hell, we stayed in the same city. He knew my address; I had stayed at the same address since I was born. My mother never stopped him from seeing or having a relationship with me, yet he hadn't been very active in my life. There was no doubt that I was his daughter. I looked just like him, so there was no way that he could deny me as his flesh and blood.

"You look like you grew taller since the last time I saw you. How you been?"

"I'm good," I replied.

"How you been doing in school?"

"I stayed on the honor roll the whole year."

"That's way better than I did. My teachers knew I had no chance of graduating. I thought you would end up attending Northwestern," Tony replied.

"I have to go," I said.

"Esha, I can drive you home. Let's go get something to eat first," Tony said.

I then got into his older Ford pickup truck, and we went to have lunch at a Coney Island restaurant. As we sat in the booth, Tony said, "I'm proud of you for keeping those grades up. What college do you plan to go to?"

"I plan to go to cosmetology school and open a hair salon one day," I replied.

"Good shit. You got that from Simone. She was hustling, doing hair in high school. How is she? Is she still with that dude? I think his name is Eric," Tony said as he ate one of his fries.

"No. They broke up two years ago. She has a new boyfriend now."

"He seemed like a good dude. Shit, that ain't none of my business. You barely ate. You good? You need me to send the food back?"

I replied, "I haven't seen you in two years. Even before that, I would see you ever so often. You haven't been much of a father to me. Why is that?"

"I knew this was coming. Esha, let me keep it one hundred, and I'm not making excuses. I was seventeen when Simone had you..."

"She was seventeen as well," I replied as I cut him off.

"Esha, let me finish. I was seventeen, and I was a young and dumb nigga, who wasn't ready to take on the responsibilities of fatherhood. I was never in a relationship with Simone; we didn't have plans to get married, and there was no love or feelings between us. I dropped outta school, still ran the streets, and was so focused on getting money the fast way. I acted like I was too good to get a minimum wage gig, not caring that I had a baby girl to feed. I stayed doing dumb shit and kept getting locked up. I remember coming to visit you. You had to be six or seven. It was Christmas Day, and I remember seeing the Christmas tree and all the decorations in the living room. You had Christmas presents everywhere. I bought you a cheap-ass baby doll from Shoppers World. I gave it to you, and you tossed that shit to the side and played with the other Christmas toys. You barely knew me. You had a life that I couldn't give you. Simone was with Eric, y'all seemed like a happy family, and I just stayed outta the way. That's no excuse for doing what I did."

"It's not," I replied.

"I can't get back the times and milestones that I missed, but I'm here now. I got myself a gig. I work at a mechanic shop, fixing cars. I got an apartment on the Eastside. I ain't got much, and I might not be able to give you everything you want, but I can give you what I can and make sure you have the things you need," Tony said.

"Okay."

"You look just like my mama," Tony said.

"I heard that she died a few years ago. I'm sorry to hear that," I replied.

"Yeah, cancer is a bad mothafucka. I don't wish that shit on my worst enemy. I miss her. Losing her made me get my shit together and realize how short life really is. I'm glad that we chopped it up today. I promise to do better this time," Tony replied.

After we left the restaurant, Tony took me home, and I asked, "Are you coming in?"

"I'm straight. Simone might not be too happy to see me. Maybe next time," Tony said.

"Bye."

"See you later, Esha."

Simone was styling her client's hair and asked, "How was the last day of school?"

"I'm just glad school is out," I replied.

"Ayesha is smart as hell," Simone bragged to her client.

"Daddy came up to the school. We had lunch at Coney Island, and he dropped me off here," I said.

Simone replied, "Tony came and picked you up from school?"

"Yeah."

"Girl, Ayesha's daddy is a sorry-ass mothafucka. This nigga hasn't seen her in two fucking years," Simone told her client.

"Why didn't we go to his mom's funeral? She was my grandma," I said.

"She was a deadbeat like her fucking son, that's why. When Tony was locked up, she bought a few packs of diapers, maybe some clothes, and that's it. She made no effort to pick you up on the weekends, come to any of your birthday parties, or any of your school ceremonies," Simone replied.

"We talked about why he hasn't been very active in my life."

"Niggas can make all the excuses in the world of why they can be a deadbeat, but women can't do that shit. We don't get to make no fucking excuses," Simone replied.

"I know that's right," Simone's client said.

"I can count on one hand how many times he stepped up to help with anything for the past fifteen years. I got four kids, and I don't make excuses; I make shit happen. Shit, I wish I could be a fucking deadbeat sometimes. It's funny how he can walk away from his responsibilities and pick and choose when the fuck he wanna play daddy."

"Ma, he promised that he would do better this time."

"You have no idea how many times I begged this nigga to pick you up. I begged him to come see you; I begged him when you needed clothes, shoes, and money for field trips. This nigga would always tell me that he would help me out, but never came through. I remember when you got sick years ago, and he couldn't even bring you one fucking bottle of cough medicine. His promises don't mean shit to me, Ayesha."

"Ma, don't you think you should forgive him and leave the past behind?"

"Ayesha, it ain't that simple. Until you know what it's like to be a single mother and not get help and support from the other mothafucka who helped you create a child, you can't tell me shit."

"Since school is out, I'm putting your butt to work this summer. You can start by helping me clean these greens," Auntie Angie said as she prepared to clean collard greens in her kitchen. "Simone told me that you saw Tony yesterday."

"Yeah. She was tripping, and she's still bitter," I replied.

"Maybe you need to see things from Simone's point of view. Show some empathy and be more understanding. It takes two to tangle. It ain't fair for two people to lay up with each other and make a child, but only one takes on all the responsibilities of raising that child. Now, I've never had children of my own, but I know it ain't easy raising them without a father," Auntie Angie said.

Being a Black single mother can be hard because of social, economic, and systemic factors. Let's start with economic disparity. Black single mothers often face lower income levels and reduced access to quality employment opportunities, making it hard to provide for their children's basic needs, including housing, food, and education. Systemic racism and discrimination also add fuel to the fire. Black mothers face a higher chance of encountering biases in health care, education, and the criminal justice system, affecting their ability to ensure their children receive fair treatment and equal opportunities. Balancing the demands of parenting four children alone can also be emotionally and physically draining, leading to high levels of stress and exhaustion. The lack of a co-parent to share responsibilities can be overwhelming, leaving little time for self-care or personal pursuits. I didn't understand Simone's frustration then, but I get it now.

CHAPTER 7

Family Feud

I woke up to a loud knock on the door.

"Who is it?"

"Child Protective Services," a female voice replied.

I whispered to myself, *"What the fuck?"*

"One moment," I replied.

"Ma, wake up! CPS is at the door!" Simone woke up and rushed to get dressed, and I rushed to get the dirty dishes out of the sink, wiped the coffee table, and picked up Elijah's and Aaliyah's toys off the living room floor. Here's what may have led to an unexpected visit with CPS.

Simone yelled at Dame, "You must think I'm fucking stupid! You out here fucking other bitches and got me out here looking stupid as fuck!"

"Man, I ain't got time for this shit today!"

Simone yelled, "You ain't going nowhere! Who is she this time?"

"Bitch, stop fucking playing with me and move!"

Simone pushed Dame and said, "Who you calling a bitch?"

"Simone, you got one more mothafucking time to touch me, and I'ma fuck you up," Dame threatened.

I sat in my room, doing Imani's hair, and said, "I wish they both shut the fuck up."

"Me too," Imani replied.

"Pass me the beeswax and the spritz," I told Imani.

"I don't like it when they fight," Elijah said as he entered our room.

"I know," I said to Elijah.

"I'm scared," Aaliyah said as she held her baby doll.

"Leelee, don't be scared. Everything will be okay, and guess what? You get to eat all the cake and ice cream you want at the party today," I said as I hugged Aaliyah, trying to cheer her up.

It was the day of Imani and Elijah's joint birthday party. Their birthdays are six days apart—Imani's on June 23rd and Elijah's on June 17th—so each year, they celebrate together on the same day. The party took place at the park on 12th Street and Delaware. Typically, the house would be excited on such occasions, but Simone and Dame's toxic behavior was killing the vibe. It was not uncommon for Simone and Dame to fight, and it got physical at times. They would start by arguing; she would put her hands on him, he would hit her, and they would fight like cats and dogs and fuck like rabbits as if nothing ever happened. One time, the fight between them got so bad that Auntie Angie called the police. Simone was so pissed at Auntie Angie for calling the police on Dame. The police never came, and if they did, Simone would've denied what really happened. I was spending the night at Kierra's one night, and when I got home, Imani told me that Dame pulled a gun out on Simone and threatened to kill her during one of their altercations. Imani had gotten so scared that she urinated on herself. If any of us intervened, Simone would say, *"Stay outta grown folks' business and stay in a child's place!"* They were undeniably the most toxic couple ever.

"Fuck you, Dame! Leave! You ain't nothing but a liar and a cheating-ass mothafucka!"

"Believe what the fuck you wanna believe," Dame said before slamming the door and leaving.

The party had started, the weather was sunny and beautiful, and everyone seemed to enjoy themselves. The picnic area at the park, underneath the shed, was beautifully decorated with balloons and other party decorations. Like every year, Simone bought two birthday cakes. Imani had a Bratz cake, and Elijah had a Spider-Man cake. Simone and Auntie Angie served grilled hot dogs, hamburgers, chips, and pop to the party guests.

"Sister Angie, can I get one of them dogs?" Tiny said as she asked Auntie Angie for a hot dog.

"Sure. Here. Take two instead and some chips and pop for you as well," Auntie Angie said.

Tiny asked, "You got ten dollars I can hold?"

"Charlene, I'm not giving you ten dollars to buy that poison."

"I'm clean now," Tiny replied.

"You know that's a lie. Baby, I'm praying for you, but I'm not giving you ten dollars." Auntie Angie said.

"God bless you, Sister Angie," Tiny smiled and said as she stumbled away.

"Charlene needs to get herself together. Those girls of hers are running wild while she's out messing with that dope," Auntie Angie said.

"I used to look up to Tiny. She was so pretty and always wore a mink around the hood, riding around with ballers. I wanted to be like her so bad," Simone said.

"And you see how she ended up. Those ballers got her hooked on that poison, and you'll end up the same way, messing around with Damien," Auntie Angie said to Simone.

"Auntie, please. I smoke a little weed sometimes, but I don't smoke crack. Crack is wack."

"But you lay up with the man who sells that poison to Charlene, Simone. I heard all that fussing this morning. It sounded like trouble in paradise between the two of you, as always."

"It's nobody's business what goes on between me and Dame."

Minutes later, Eric pulled up in his Jeep Grand Cherokee.

"It's good to see you, Eric," I said, greeting him as he opened the passenger door for a brown-skinned woman who rocked a Nia Long pixie cut.

"Ayesha, I want you to meet someone. This is my wife, Tanya. Tanya, this is Ayesha."

"Nice to meet you," I said to Tanya.

"Nice to meet you too, Ayesha. I've heard so much about you," Tanya replied.

"Eric, what is she doing here?" Simone asked out of the blue, pointing at Tanya.

"Don't start, Simone. Elijah and Aaliyah like Tanya. She's just here to celebrate like everyone else," Eric said to Simone.

"This is a family affair, and she ain't family," Simone said.

"She's my wife, Simone," Eric said.

"Maybe I should leave, Eric," Tanya said.

"Yeah, you should," Simone said to Tanya.

"No, you're not going anywhere. You're my wife; this is my son's party, and you're a part of his life now. You have every right to be here," Eric told Tanya.

"You got some nerve, bringing this raggedy-ass bitch here!"

"Excuse me? You will not disrespect me," Tanya said.

"Do something about it then, bitch," Simone said.

"Eric, I will not stoop to the level of this ghetto-ass hood rat," Tanya said.

"This hood rat will fuck you up!" Simone yelled.

Eric then got in the middle of Simone and Tanya, preventing them from swinging at each other, when Auntie Angie intervened, "Stop it! This is embarrassing! That's enough! Don't do this in front of all these children!"

"Auntie, I don't want her here!"

"You got some nerve, Simone," Auntie Angie said. "She's a guest, and that's not how we treat our guests! Hey, Eric and Tanya. We were just getting ready to cut the cakes. Tanya, you can put the gifts on the table and enjoy the party," Auntie Angie continued.

"You know, Simone, I heard about your thug-ass boyfriend and how he puts his hands on you in front of our children. That's not the type of environment that they should be in. I'm going for full custody of Elijah and Aaliyah," Eric threatened.

"Michigan is a MOTHER state. They ain't giving you full custody, but you can go ahead and try," Simone said.

"That's enough! Eric, go over there with Tanya," Auntie Angie said.

After the party ended, Dawn was fighting Tiny.

"You stole my money, crackhead-ass bitch!" Dawn yelled as she pounded on Tiny, snatching off Tiny's wig.

"Dawn, stop it! How dare you talk to her like that and raise a hand to that woman? She gave you life," Auntie Angie said.

"Miss Angie, this bitch stole three hundred dollars from me!"

"Dawn, the Bible says, *Honor your father and your mother, so that you may live long in the land our Lord is giving you,*" Auntie Angie said.

"I don't care! I would rather have a dead mother than this bitch! How can you expect me to honor the same mother who stole from me? This is the same mother who sold me to grown-ass men to smoke crack pipes! This is the same mother who left me alone to starve! This is the same mother who left me to raise my sister, and you expect me to honor her? I would rather die than honor her!"

"Dawn, you don't mean that," Auntie Angie said.

"Don't tell me what I don't mean! Are you gonna give me my money back, huh, Miss Angie? Where were you when we were alone? Where were you when we needed food? Where were you when our lights got cut off? If it weren't for the food pantries at Everlasting Grace, we wouldn't have had anything to eat. You stopped my sister from spending the night with Ayesha when my sister used to go over there. All Talisha wanted was a hot meal and a warm bed. You've always looked down on us. That's not how Christians treat people. Stay outta this!"

"Auntie, leave them alone. This has nothing to do with us," Simone said to Auntie Angie.

A few days after Imani and Elijah's birthday party, I did a quick cleanup, and Simone let the woman from CPS in.

"My name is Patricia Carter, and I work for Child Protective Services. Are you Simone Jones?"

"Yes, I am. Can I ask, why are you here?"

"Miss Jones, I have received concerns about the safety of the children in this household. I must investigate those concerns. To my understanding, you have four children: Ayesha Jones, Imani Jones, Elijah Smith, and Aaliyah Smith, ages fifteen, thirteen, nine, and six, correct?"

Simone replied, "Yes. Miss Carter, can I ask who called CPS on me?"

"I am unable to disclose that information, Miss Jones. There are some concerns regarding domestic disputes in the household between you and your boyfriend, whose name is Damien. Is that correct?"

"Yes, but as far as the domestic disputes…"

"And is Dame his alias?"

"Yes," Simone replied.

"It has been brought to my attention that you and Damien have domestic disputes in front of the children quite often, and the children are in fear when these disputes occur."

"We argue and yell from time to time, but he ain't slapping, choking, punching, and kicking me all over the place."

"Have the children witnessed any of these disputes?"

"They may have," Simone replied.

"Is Damien employed?"

"He has a job."

"And what is his place of employment?"

"I'm not sure," Simone said.

"Miss Jones, are you telling me that you don't know where your boyfriend works?"

"My mind is all over the place right now. I can't think straight," Simone replied.

"There are concerns that Damien sells drugs for a living. Miss Jones, I'm going to be honest with you. The children's safety in this home is quite concerning, based on the allegations of domestic violence and illegal drug activity. I'm going to issue a safety plan. Your boyfriend Damien is not allowed in the home until the case is closed, and there is no evidence proving that these children are in danger. If you fail to comply with the safety plan, the children will be removed from your home. Here are some resources for women and children who are victims of domestic violence," Patricia said, handing Simone a piece of paper.

Patricia then did a walkthrough around the house to see if there was enough food in the home, running water, and if we had proper sleeping arrangements, and left shortly after.

"Ma, are you okay?"

"I know who the fuck did this," Simone said before she stormed downstairs to Auntie Angie's duplex.

Imani asked me, "You think Auntie Angie did this?"

"I don't know," I replied.

"Why the hell are you beating on my damn door like you're the police?"

"Auntie, I know it was you who called CPS on me!"

"I didn't call no CPS on you," Auntie Angie replied.

"Then who else did? You hate Dame so much, you would go that far! You told them about the fights and that he sold drugs!"

"I may not like Damien, but I wouldn't dare put you at risk of having those babies taken from you. I'm sorry that happened to you.

Come here. Everything will be fine. Pray about it and talk to God," Auntie Angie said while she hugged Simone, who cried in Auntie Angie's arms.

Two days later, Eric dropped Elijah and Aaliyah off at home after they spent a few days at his house, and Simone confronted Eric. Eric did say that he was going for full custody of Elijah and Aaliyah, so pinning a CPS case on Simone would strengthen his case and increase his chances of winning the custody battle.

Simone said to Eric on the porch, "You dirty mothafucka."

"Kids, go in the house. Mommy and Daddy need to talk," Eric said to Elijah and Aaliyah.

"I know you called CPS on me. It had to be you. It's funny how you threatened me with full custody, and CPS popped up at my house. How ironic is that?"

"Simone, I did not call CPS on you. I don't know what you're talking about."

"That's what you say. See you in court," Simone replied.

A few weeks later, the CPS case came back, stating there was not enough evidence to prove any of the allegations, and the case was closed. However, the person who gave CPS the tips remained a mystery.

CHAPTER 8

Fifteen & Pregnant

"What does it say?"

"It has two lines," I said as I read the pregnancy test in my bathroom.

"Fuck! That's the third pregnancy test that came out positive! Shit! I'm so fucked right now!"

The summer of 2004 was one hell of a summer.

"Kierra, I told you that you and TJ should always use condoms."

"I'm fucking pregnant. I can't believe this shit. I don't know what to do."

Summer vacation was going by so fast. It seemed like the last day of school was yesterday. It was August, back-to-school was around the corner, and I thought the drama stayed at school. I was wrong.

"Kierra, regardless of what decision you make, you need to see a doctor. Does TJ know?"

"No, I haven't told him yet. My mama is gonna be pissed and will probably kick me out. I don't wanna tell her. I have to go and figure something out. I'll see you later," Kierra said before she left.

"Call me when you get home," I said.

"Ayesha Nicole Jones! Wake your mothafucking ass up!" Simone yelled the next morning.

"Ma, it's seven-thirty in the morning," I replied in a sleepy tone.

"You got something you need to tell me?" Simone asked.

"No, what are you talking about?"

"I found this pregnancy test in the bathroom trash can! You got some explaining to do," Simone said.

"It's not mine," I replied.

Simone replied, "Then it must be yours, Imani!"

"I promise to God, I'm not pregnant," Imani said.

"Well, it ain't Aaliyah's, and it ain't mine, so whose is it? Somebody better tell me something!" Simone yelled.

"It's Kierra's. Kierra is pregnant," I replied.

Imani said, "Ayesha's gonna be a godmama."

Simone said, "Hush, Imani!" Simone continued, "I'm not surprised. Does Renee know?"

"No."

"Well, I'm telling her," Simone said.

"Ma, please don't," I pleaded.

"What type of friend and mother would I be if I didn't let Renee know that Kierra is with child? I don't know why I let you hang with that girl. She's too damn grown for her age," Simone said before walking out of the room.

I went to Kierra's house the next day.

"Come on in. Simone told me Kierra's secret. I knew it; that dumb bitch. I took her to the clinic yesterday, and this bitch is seven weeks pregnant. I'm taking her to get an abortion tomorrow. I'm glad I ain't paying for it," Renee said.

"Girl, I'm sorry. My mama found the pregnancy test in the trash can. She thought I was pregnant and went nuts. I had to tell her the truth," I said to Kierra while we were in her room.

"It's okay. TJ gave me the money for the abortion," Kierra said.

"Where did he get the money from?"

"He got it from his dad," Kierra replied.

"Miss Renee said that she was taking you to get an abortion tomorrow. If you don't mind, I'll go with you," I said.

"I don't mind. I'll be glad when this shit is over with. I'm sick of hearing my mama's fucking mouth. You have no idea how many dumb bitches, slut bitches, and hoes I've been called today. I don't wanna deal with no crying-ass baby, change shitty-ass diapers, and get fat as hell anyway. I'm glad that I'm killing it," Kierra said.

"Don't say it like that, Kierra!"

"It's true! Fuck this shit," Kierra said.

"What time is your appointment tomorrow?"

"Tomorrow morning at ten," Kierra said.

"I'll be there to support you. You're my best friend, and I'll always be here for you," I said.

The next morning, we arrived at Northwest Women's Center, and Kierra was about to have her abortion.

"Kierra Johnson?" The medical assistant said as we sat in the waiting room.

Kierra walked into the back room for her procedure. I continued to wait in the waiting room with Renee.

"Don't be like Kierra. You're way smarter than she is. Don't let any of these niggas get you pregnant. I tried to tell her over and over again. What if that nigga didn't give her the money for the abortion? I can't afford another mouth to feed. She can't take care of a baby. She can't even take care of herself. Stay away from these niggas, go to college, and get married before you start having babies, Ayesha."

"I will," I replied.

"I had an abortion when I was fifteen, except I was pregnant by my uncle, not some boy I liked. My uncle had been molesting me for years, and it got worse as I got older. People in the family knew what my uncle was doing to me, and they swept that shit under the rug. They acted as if nothing happened. They still treated him like family. That sick bastard came to all the family barbeques and holiday parties. Everybody just turned a blind eye to what was going on, and they knew. When I married Kenny and we had Junior, I was so happy to be having a boy. When I was pregnant with Kierra, I was so fucking furious. Kenny wanted a girl, but I didn't wanna bring a girl into this sick-ass world. Every time I look at her, it's a reminder of what I went through. When you look at Kierra, you see those curves, and she's so beautiful. I was built like that at her age and ended up getting fucked by my own family. I didn't want the same shit that happened to me to happen to my daughter. I still don't speak to my family. I never told Kierra any of this stuff. It ain't that easy to talk about," Renee said as a tear came down her cheek.

Renee, having endured trauma, resorted to coping mechanisms such as excessive drinking instead of seeking the appropriate treatment. Whether alcohol or drugs, many individuals grappling with substance abuse have faced trauma stemming from various sources, including rape, molestation, the loss of loved ones, near-death experiences like car accidents or gunshot incidents, and military service-related trauma. These substances become a means of dealing with the pain. Kierra harbored resentment towards her mother for years due to her drinking habits, unaware of the depth of her mother's suffering. Renee, in turn, directed her pent-up anguish towards Kierra over the years, a manifestation of the profound damage inflicted by her past pain. The adage *hurt people hurt people* emphasizes that individuals in pain may inadvertently cause harm to others. Had Renee received proper treatment, such as therapy and spiritual counseling, to aid in her healing process, her relationship with Kierra could have been more positive. Despite my desire to share Renee's revelations with Kierra, I recognized that it wasn't my place to divulge someone else's personal story.

When Kierra finally finished the procedure and walked into the waiting room, she looked lightheaded and uncomfortable. I approached her and asked, "How do you feel?"

"I'll never get another abortion again. It felt like bad period cramps, but way worse, and I'm still cramping. I'm in so much pain." Kierra said.

When we got in the car, Renee yelled the whole ride home, "I hope you learned a fucking lesson! I had to call off work for this bullshit! Kenny is rolling over in his damn grave! I'm so pissed, I could strangle you right now! That nigga ain't got no job, and neither do you, and you two dumb mothafuckas out here making babies! You can't even buy period pads for yourself; how the fuck can you buy some diapers? I guess you thought I was supposed to take care of that little bastard. You got me fucked up! I'm still taking care of you! If you can't fuck responsibly, then you don't need to be fucking! The next time you pull some shit like this, I'm putting you out on the streets! If you're grown enough to fuck and get pregnant, then you're grown enough to get the fuck out!"

"I wish she shut the fuck up," Kierra said to me as we sat in the back seat.

"You got my damn blood pressure up. I need to stop and get me a drink," Renee said.

"You always need a drink," Kierra mumbled.

The next day, I decided to enjoy a humid summer day in the pool at the Joseph Walker Williams Recreation Center. On my way home, I ran into Talisha, who was carrying a pizza from Little Caesars, and I said, "Hey."

"So now you wanna speak to me? You always act fake when you're around Kierra," Talisha replied.

"I'm sorry for teasing you at the park that day."

"Yeah, right. You wouldn't be apologizing if Kierra was around, so stop with that fake-ass shit. I guess you're too ashamed to be around Crackhead Tiny's daughter," Talisha said.

"Is it true? Did you let Zayvion, Cory, Peanut, and Tez have sex with you?"

"It's not what you think or what you heard," Talisha replied.

The story that Talisha told me was disturbing. Talisha went over to Zayvion's house to have sex with Tez, and after she had sex with Tez, Talisha experienced something that no woman should ever have to experience.

"My turn," Zayvion said after he walked into the room.

Talisha shouted as she prepared to put on her shirt, standing in her bra and panties, "Fuck you, Zayvion, get the fuck out! I'm getting dressed!"

"You got some nice titties," Zayvion said as he squeezed one of her breasts.

"Nigga, don't fucking touch me!" Talisha yelled and slapped Zayvion.

"Stupid-ass bitch!" Zayvion said as he pushed Talisha onto the bed and got on top of her.

"Get the fuck off me, Zayvion! Tez, get him off me! Tez!" Talisha yelled as Tez stood and watched.

"You know you want this dick, stop playing. Tez said you would let us all fuck," Zayvion said when he pulled her panties down, inserted his penis in her vagina, and started thrusting.

"No! Stop! Get off me!" Talisha cried and screamed.

Once Zayvion was done, Cory walked into the room with Peanut and said, "It's my turn now. I want that pussy from the back," Cory said as he pulled his pants down to his ankles and turned Talisha on her stomach.

"Cory, stop! Please," Talisha cried.

"Shut the fuck up, and take this dick," Cory said as he pushed Talisha's face down and proceeded to pound her from behind.

"Bro, she likes that shit. These hoes like it rough," Zayvion said to his big brother Cory.

"Your turn, Peanut. It's time for you to get some pussy, little nigga," Cory said after he was done having sex with Talisha.

"I'm straight," Peanut replied nervously.

"Nigga, I know you ain't scared. Stop being a bitch, you pussy-ass nigga!" Cory yelled.

"Man, y'all niggas tripping. I'm out," Peanut said before he left.

"I knew that nigga Peanut was a faggot," Cory said. "You can get dressed and leave now. Thanks for the pussy. I couldn't wait to fuck your pretty ass. That little pussy was tight. Tez said you had some good pussy. I had to see for myself. Oh, and tell your crackhead-ass mama I'll give her a rock for some head. Cheer up, you know you liked that shit," Cory said as Talisha cried.

"Oh my God, Talisha! They raped you! Why didn't you tell the police?"

"If I told the police, I would be known as a snitch. Snitches get stitches in the hood. They would all go to jail, especially Cory. Cory is twenty-four, and he's the only one who's not a minor. The rumor around the hood is that I had sex with Tez, Zayvion, Cory, and Peanut. Peanut was the only one who had mercy on me and never touched me. I thought Tez liked me. He was supposed to be my boyfriend and didn't even try to help me. Tez set me up. I'll never forgive him for that," Talisha said.

"I'm sorry."

"Don't be sorry. That wasn't the first time I got raped. You don't know what it's like to be passed around to strangers and be sold for crack. My mama will let grown men do what Zayvion, Cory, and Tez did to me for a glass dick. She did the same thing to Dawn," Talisha replied.

"Talisha, is there anything that I can do?"

"Keep quiet. Don't tell anyone. Let people think what they want about me. I gotta get home," Talisha said.

Talisha was only fifteen and had already been raped several times, and who knows the impact that it might've had on her mentally. Sexual abuse can affect people on emotional, psychological, and interpersonal levels. Survivors often grapple with overwhelming feelings of guilt and shame, even though they bear no responsibility for the abuse. Fear and anxiety can become constants in their lives, potentially leading to anxiety disorders and panic attacks. Depression, coupled with plummeting self-esteem, may set in, making it challenging to find joy or self-worth. Anger and irritability can emerge as a response to trauma, further complicating emotional well-being. Survivors might experience PTSD with its debilitating symptoms, such as flashbacks, nightmares, and avoidance behaviors. Some people may dissociate or depersonalize, detaching from their bodies as a coping mechanism. These experiences can erode trust in others, resulting in difficulties in forming healthy relationships. Isolation may become a refuge from judgment, and sexual and intimacy issues can strain partnerships. Physical health may also deteriorate, with psychosomatic symptoms surfacing, and some survivors resort to substance abuse as a means of escape. The long-term consequences can impact adult life, including relationships and careers, and survivors may be at risk of re-victimization. It's important to emphasize that recovery is attainable through therapy, support, and understanding, offering survivors a path to healing and rebuilding their lives.

I felt so bad for misjudging and teasing Talisha. Talisha and I were best friends when we were younger. I met Talisha before I met Kierra, and I had known Talisha since kindergarten. Kierra and I would have sleepovers at my house, playing with Barbies, watching movies, pretending that we were TLC and Destiny's Child, and singing and dancing to their songs. Simone would always do Talisha's hair for free and would give Talisha a lot of my hand-me-downs. As we got older, Talisha and I grew apart. One of the reasons was that Kierra and Talisha didn't get along; they fell out over some boy they both liked. Talisha was right about me being embarrassed to hang out with her. I shouldn't have given a fuck what anyone thought. She lived in an unstable, chaotic home environment characterized by neglect, unpredictability, and emotional turmoil. As a friend, I should've shown her empathy, taken some time to self-reflect, understood her perspective, validated her feelings and emotions, respected her privacy and boundaries, and encouraged her to seek counseling. From that day forward, I decided not to allow Kierra or anyone else to tease Talisha or call her names.

CHAPTER 9

Tragedy

I was starting school in two weeks. I kept in contact with Tony regularly, and he took me to Rainbow to buy some school clothes. I was happy to have a better relationship with my dad. I enjoyed my time shopping, eating lunch, and spending time with him. It seemed like a good day. The weather was beautiful, warm, and sunny, and no one would've predicted what just happened. When we pulled up to my house, there was a crowd of people on the block. When I got out of the car, the first thing I noticed was Dame's dead body and Aaliyah's pink bike on the lawn.

"Somebody help me!" Simone screamed.

I pushed through the crowd of people and saw Simone holding Aaliyah in her arms. Aaliyah's yellow Rocawear shirt was covered in blood, her eyes rolled to the back of her head, and blood was coming from her mouth. My shopping bags fell on the concrete when I dropped them. My body went numb, I couldn't move, and everything felt like it was in slow motion.

"We can't wait on no ambulance! Somebody gotta drive her to the hospital!" Auntie Angie yelled.

"I'll take her! Come on, Simone!" Tony said as Simone carried Aaliyah into Tony's truck before speeding off.

"What happened?" I asked.

"It was a drive-by shooting. Some fools drove up and started shooting at Dame. Aaliyah got caught in the crossfire and got shot. It happened right before you and Tony pulled up. I was cleaning the house, and suddenly, I heard a bunch of gunshots. I called Eric, and he's on his way here. Imani and Elijah are in my house. They're both shaken up," Auntie Angie said.

Our house turned into a whole crime scene. I remember seeing the yellow crime tape, news trucks, a white sheet being covered over Dame's dead body, police everywhere, etc. It was like a scene from a movie.

"I got here as fast as I could. Where are the kids?" Eric asked.

"Imani and Elijah are in the house," Auntie Angie replied.

"Thank God!" Eric replied.

"Simone is at the hospital with Aaliyah. Aaliyah got shot," Auntie Angie said.

"What? No, no, this can't be happening," Eric said before he went to his Jeep.

"Ayesha, go with Eric. I have to stay here and give a statement to the police," Auntie Angie said.

We arrived at the hospital unit where Simone and Tony were, and Simone was nervously pacing back and forth. We waited in the waiting room, and the doctor eventually came out with a disappointing look on his face. He talked to Simone and Eric, and whatever he said made Simone scream, "No! Not my baby!" Simone fell to the floor and cried hysterically. Tony helped her up, and she cried in Tony's arms until nurses and doctors came to comfort her. Eric then put his hands over his head, cried, and started beating his fists against the wall.

"She didn't make it. The doctors did everything they could to save her," Tony told me.

It hadn't hit me that my youngest sister just died. I was in so much shock that I couldn't shed a single tear. I couldn't believe this was happening and thought to myself, *"Maybe I'm dreaming. This is just a nightmare. I'll wake up soon. Aaliyah can't be dead. This isn't real. It can't be real. Ayesha, wake up. Wake the fuck up, Ayesha!"* I sat in a chair at the hospital for hours with a blank look on my face. I didn't speak; I barely moved; I just sat and waited for the nightmare to end.

"Let's go, Esha," Tony said.

"I watched my mama take her last breath. I saw niggas get shot and even lost a few of my niggas, but this was my first time seeing a child die. I feel sorry for Eric. The last thing he wanted to hear was that his daughter was dead. That's fucked up. I feel sorry for Simone. She'll never get over that shit," Tony said as he smoked a cigarette in his truck, as tears rolled down his face.

Hours later, I realized that my nightmare was a reality while lying on Auntie Angie's couch, watching the news. The caption said, ***"Two people killed in a drive-by shooting,"*** before Dame and Aaliyah's pictures popped up on the TV screen.

"Two people were killed in a drive-by shooting this afternoon. The shooting happened on Euclid Street on Detroit's West Side. The victims were twenty-eight-year-old Damien Evans and six-year-old Aaliyah Smith. No suspects have been arrested at this time," the news anchor said.

"Turn this mess off. The children don't know yet, and this is not how they should find out," Auntie Angie said as she turned off the TV. "I went upstairs and gave Simone a sleeping pill. I stayed with her until she fell asleep. I made Imani and Elijah stay down here for the night. They don't need to see Simone like that," Auntie Angie continued.

"Aaliyah's gone, but I haven't even cried yet."

"You're in shock. Grief doesn't always hit you right away, but it will sooner or later. Simone is gonna be devastated when she wakes up and remembers what happened to Aaliyah. Imani and Elijah... God, help me as I prepare to tell these poor babies that their sister passed away. Elijah was so worried about Aaliyah before he went to bed. Aaliyah was his partner in crime. She was sweet but sassy and always bossing Elijah around. She thought she was the oldest. I'll miss that child."

The next day, our house was surrounded by the news crew, neighbors, family, and members from our church, Everlasting Grace Baptist Church. We gathered for a balloon release and candlelight vigil to remember Aaliyah. People prayed, sang, offered condolences, brought dishes and money, and set up a makeshift memorial with teddy bears, flowers, cards, and candles near where she was shot. Simone was a mess. She cried, screamed, and still wore the same clothes she had on with Aaliyah's blood. I was the only one who didn't cry. It still didn't hit me yet.

On the day the funeral arrangements were made, Simone was still wearing the same clothes. She was taking Aaliyah's death hard. We always said that Aaliyah was Simone's favorite. Simone was tough on me and Imani because we were the oldest, and we were teenagers, but she had a soft spot for Elijah and Aaliyah, especially Aaliyah.

"Simone, would you like to change clothes?" Auntie Angie asked, looking at Simone's blood-stained clothes.

"No, I'm fine with what I have on," Simone replied.

"But baby…"

Simone interrupted Auntie Angie, "Auntie, can we just go?"

"Okay. Let's go. Imani, keep an eye on Elijah. Stay in the house and don't answer the door for nobody," Auntie Angie said.

When we got outside, a group of news reporters and cameramen were sticking cameras and microphones in our faces as Auntie Angie yelled, "Get the hell off my property! We ain't doing no damn interviews! My niece just lost her baby! Can't you see she's grieving? Have some damn respect!" We then got into Auntie Angie's car and drove to the bank, followed by a children's boutique to pick out Aaliyah's dress, and finally to the funeral home.

"We require that your loved one be dressed in long-sleeve clothing. Are you having an open-casket service?" The funeral director asked.

"Um, yes," Auntie Angie replied.

The funeral director asked, "Do you prefer a burial or cremation?"

"Cremation? I'm not fucking burning my baby. Why is that even an option?" Simone snapped.

"Simone, calm down," Auntie Angie pleaded.

"Lady, why the fuck do you keep staring at my shirt like you ain't never seen blood before? This is a funeral home. You see blood all the time," Simone said to the funeral director.

"Have you chosen which casket you want?"

"We're going with the pink and white casket," Auntie Angie replied to the funeral director.

"I can't do this shit," Simone said as she got up and walked away.

"Here's her dress. I apologize for my niece's behavior," Auntie Angie said as she handed the funeral director Aaliyah's dress.

"No need to apologize. Losing a child is hard for any parent. We understand."

"I'll go after her," I told Auntie Angie.

"Ma, I know this is hard," I said as we stood outside.

Simone cried, "My baby should be at home watching cartoons or playing with Elijah and not dead in this damn funeral home. What the fuck did I do to deserve this? God, why me? Why me?"

On the day of Aaliyah's funeral, I was still in my pajamas, sitting on the porch, looking at the makeshift memorial for Aaliyah. It was a warm and sunny day, perfect for fishing, grilling, or swimming – not for a funeral. Eric sat next to me, dressed in a black suit, and said, "Ayesha, the limo will be here in less than an hour to pick us up."

"Where's Tanya?"

"Tanya is driving to the service by herself. Tensions are high as is, so she thought that it was best to meet me at the church. Tanya and Simone aren't the best of friends, and there's no need to make today worse than it already is," Eric replied.

"I didn't go to the visitation yesterday, and I'm not going to the funeral."

"Ayesha, I know that this is very hard for you. It's hard for all of us. I wanted to die when I first saw her in that casket. I still have the school uniforms and school supplies that I bought her to start second grade. God only gave me six years with my daughter, and to be honest, I feel robbed. I'm going through a range of emotions. None of us are prepared to say our final goodbyes today. I could be angry with Simone all I want. I could blame her, blame Dame, blame God, but what good will that do? Simone and I had our issues, but I know that Simone loved Aaliyah, and she loves you, Imani, and Elijah, and she's truly devastated by this. You're the oldest, and I need you to be strong for Simone. Simone is going to need your support today. Today is rough for all of us. Aaliyah would want you there, so please, do me a favor, do your mother a favor, do your sister and brother a favor, and get dressed," Eric replied.

Aaliyah's funeral was held at Everlasting Grace Baptist Church. The church was overcrowded, surrounded by strangers who wanted to pay their respects, people from around the neighborhood, her first-grade teacher, the principal from Thirkell Elementary, family, and friends. When I walked up to the white and pink casket adorned with pink flowers, Aaliyah looked like a beautiful sleeping angel. She wore a white dress with a long-sleeved white jacket, ponytails held by white barrettes, a rhinestone tiara on her head, and teddy bears placed in her casket beside her. It was the first time I saw Aaliyah since the day she was shot, and the first time I had cried since her death. When I touched her cheek, it was cold. I touched her hand, and it was cold as well. I broke down, cried, and almost collapsed. I remember Kierra putting her arm around me and leading me back to my seat at the church as I sobbed. Simone was crying and fell to the floor when they were about to close Aaliyah's casket. Imani brought the whole church to tears when she sang Smokie Norful's *I Need You Now*.

"Now for the reading of the obituary," the pastor said.

A woman came to the front of the church, opened the obituary, and said, "Aaliyah Arielle Smith's journey began on November fifth, nineteen ninety-seven, as a precious gift to Simone Jones and Eric Smith. As the youngest among her siblings, she brought an extra dose of joy and mischief to their family adventures. Aaliyah's infectious spirit was a blend of smarts, playfulness, sweetness, and just a dash of feistiness. With a skip in her step and a sparkle in her eye, she embraced each day with enthusiasm, especially when it came to school. Aaliyah was one of the top students in her first-grade class, but beyond the classroom, Aaliyah's world was a playground of imagination. Whether she was lost in a world of make-believe with her cherished dolls, creating vibrant masterpieces with her crayons, or dancing to the beat of her own heart, her joy knew no bounds. And oh, how she loved to sing and dance! Her melodic voice filled the air with laughter and love, a sweet serenade to the joys of childhood. Aaliyah's favorite color was pink, her favorite food was pizza, and she loved watching *Finding Nemo*."

"On August twenty-third, two thousand four, as the summer breeze whispered its secrets, Aaliyah's earthly journey reached its end, as God called his precious angel back to his loving embrace. Though her time with us was fleeting, her impact was infinite, leaving a trail of love and laughter in her wake. Joined now by her beloved maternal grandparents, Clarence and Lorraine Jones, Aaliyah's spirit lives on in the hearts of those who adored her most. To her dear parents, Simone Jones and Eric Smith (Tanya), and her cherished siblings, Ayesha, Imani, and Elijah, she remains forever woven into the fabric of their lives, a reminder of the beauty of innocence and the power of love."

Aaliyah's homeroom first-grade teacher said, "Good afternoon, everyone. My name is Keisha Kimble, and for the past three years, I've had the privilege of being a first-grade teacher at Thirkell Elementary School. Today, as we gather to honor Aaliyah's memory, I find myself grappling with the unexpectedness of this moment. Aaliyah was more than just a student to me; she was a bright presence in our classroom, always eager to help and participate. Her vibrant spirit and contagious enthusiasm enriched our learning environment every single day. I knew that with her intelligence, she would be a Cass Tech, Renaissance, or King graduate, or with her desire to be the star of the show, she would be a graduate of Detroit School of Arts. Aaliyah's kindness, intelligence, and impeccable manners left a lasting impression on me and everyone she encountered. She was a shining example of goodness and grace. While her physical presence may no longer be with us, her spirit will forever remain in our hearts. Aaliyah, you will be deeply missed, and your memory will continue to inspire us all."

Her funeral service was filled with tearful goodbyes and heartfelt remarks. Our somber procession made its way to the tranquil grounds of the Detroit Memorial Gardens Cemetery. As we laid Aaliyah to rest, surrounded by a sea of flowers and solemn silence, the weight of our loss felt heavier than ever. After the ceremony, we gathered at the Northwest Activity Center for the repass, seeking solace in the company of friends and family. The atmosphere was one of bittersweet reminiscence, mingled with the comfort of shared memories and shared grief. Aaliyah's funeral was orchestrated with meticulous care, and every detail was carefully arranged to honor her memory with the grace and dignity befitting a princess. But amidst the solemnity and ceremony, the undeniable truth remained: our beloved Aaliyah was gone, leaving an irreplaceable void in our lives. For Simone, Aaliyah's passing was more than just the loss of a cherished family member; it was the shattering of a piece of her own identity. In the wake of

Aaliyah's death, Simone found herself grappling with a profound sense of emptiness.

CHAPTER 10

Aftermath

"Eric, you don't have to do this," Auntie Angie pleaded.

"Simone missed the hearing; therefore, the judge granted me custody."

"That girl just buried her child two days ago. Be reasonable."

"We both buried a child two days ago. What else am I supposed to do? Elijah is telling me that he's scared to live here because he's afraid of getting shot like his sister. He's been having nightmares about it. My son is traumatized."

"Simone already lost one child; you don't need to take Elijah away from her," Auntie Angie said.

"Elijah isn't dead; he's just coming to live with me. Simone isn't well and mentally capable of caring for Elijah right now, and you and I both know that."

"I can help take care of Elijah, Eric," Auntie Angie said.

"Auntie, you've done enough over the years, and I appreciate it, but Elijah is my son and my responsibility. Look, I'm not trying to cause any chaos; I'm just a concerned father doing what's best. I'm not trying to hurt Simone any more than she's already been hurt, and when she gets well, maybe we can work out some arrangements in the future. What would you do if you were in my shoes?"

"You're just doing what's best for that baby, and I can't even argue with that. Make sure you bring Elijah to visit us," Auntie Angie said as she hugged Eric.

"You know I will, Auntie."

"Bye, Esha. I love you," Elijah hugged me.

"I love you, too," I replied.

"Tell Imani I love her," Elijah said.

"I will, Elijah. Be good."

I stood on the porch with Auntie Angie, watching Eric and Elijah drive away, when Auntie Angie asked, "Where's Imani?"

"She stormed out before Elijah left. She was upset about Elijah leaving. Knowing her, she's probably at the park," I replied.

"Elijah is in good hands. He's with his daddy, and Miss Tanya is a nice lady," Auntie Angie said.

"I don't care, Auntie Angie."

"Well, excuse me. Did I say something wrong?"

"Eric just took Elijah away as if my mom isn't already devastated!"

"Ayesha, Elijah is scared to death. That baby needs proper nurturing, and Simone hasn't been right since Aaliyah died. Has she eaten anything today?"

"No. She's been in her room. She only comes out when she needs to use the bathroom. Not much has changed," I replied.

"I'm making some chicken noodle soup. I'll bring Simone some. She needs to put something other than liquor in her stomach," Auntie Angie said.

I remember being so mad at Eric for taking Elijah away. When Eric picked up Elijah, I didn't speak to Eric at all. At the time, I didn't think that Eric was doing the right thing, and I thought that Eric was being spiteful toward my mom. Prior to Aaliyah's death, Simone wasn't perfect, but she was never a downright unfit mother. If Simone had shown up to the court hearing, I don't think the judge would've awarded Eric custody. Things may be different now, but twenty years ago, it wasn't very easy for a mother to lose custody of her children in Wayne County. If a mother lost custody, it was because she was a drug addict or very abusive.

I went into the house and into Simone's bedroom to check on her, and she was lying in her bed with her back facing the door. I said, "Ma, there's no easy way to say this. Eric came and got Elijah."

Simone didn't reply. She just continued lying in her bed.

"Auntie Angie is bringing you some soup later. You know she makes the best homemade chicken noodle soup."

Simone remained silent.

"Well, I'll be checking on you. I love you," I said as I kissed Simone on the cheek.

I heard her crying as soon as I closed her door. I had never seen my mother so broken. She cried all the time, blamed herself, wished death upon herself, and cursed God for what happened. There were incidents where she would wake up in the middle of the night and come into our room looking for Aaliyah, and when she saw Aaliyah's empty bed, she would break down. Simone didn't care about how she looked. Her hair was always a mess; she had bags under her eyes, and she walked around wearing dingy T-shirts, sweats, and pajamas. Even her hygiene became a problem. She was not the woman I had always known to be stylish and glamorous.

What made matters worse was that Simone was drinking heavily. Simone wasn't a big drinker before all this. She'd have a drink on special occasions or with Dame sometimes, and they'd end up having drunk sex. But Simone always made it clear she didn't want to become addicted to alcohol because it could mess up how you look, age you faster, and harm your body. Simone was careful not to mess up her looks or health. She never smoked cigarettes, hated them, actually, and said that cigarettes killed Granddaddy Slick. Simone was a hairstylist, and she was really good at it. She never wanted to be drunk or high while working on her clients' hair. After Aaliyah died, whenever her friends came over, they brought her alcohol to try to cheer her up, and that's how her drinking habit started.

When someone passes away, family and friends often offer support by saying things like, *"If you need anything, just let me know."* They're there for you during the tough times, offering comfort and help. But once the funeral is over, it can feel like that support disappears. Visits dwindle, the phone stops ringing, and people go back to their own lives. That's exactly what happened after Aaliyah's funeral.

Simone usually cooked and kept the house clean, but I took on the responsibilities of cooking and cleaning lately. I had struggled with Aaliyah's death as well. I would only go upstairs to cook and clean, but I couldn't sleep up there. I shared a room with Aaliyah, and not seeing her there anymore was devastating, so I slept at Auntie Angie's.

Auntie Angie said, "I got Simone to eat some soup. I'm glad that I was able to get her to put something in her stomach. I didn't see Imani upstairs. It's almost eleven o'clock at night! She left before Eric came and got Elijah, and that was three in the afternoon. Where the hell is she?"

"She's not upstairs?"

"No!"

I sat on the porch with Auntie Angie. Imani came home at almost midnight. A sober Simone would've beat Imani's ass for that.

"You must have a job. That's the only excuse you should have for coming home this late. Where the hell were you?" Auntie Angie questioned Imani.

"I was with my friends," Imani replied.

"You are supposed to be in the house when these streetlights come on. You know better," Auntie Angie said.

"But it ain't no school tomorrow," Imani said.

"I don't give a damn! You ain't grown, Imani!"

"You ain't my mama," Imani replied.

"Little girl, what did you just say to me? Who the hell do you think used to whup Simone's ass when she was little? I'll whup yours just like I whupped Simone. Get in the house! Now!"

I followed Imani upstairs and said, "Imani, what is wrong with you? You can't be talking back to Auntie Angie."

"Auntie Angie ain't my mama."

"She's your great-aunt, and you should respect your elders, Imani."

"Auntie Angie hates me. She treats you way better than me."

"She loves you."

"Not as much as she loves you," Imani replied.

"You can't just come home anytime you want, Imani. You have a curfew."

"But you get to leave and go to Kierra's house anytime you want."

"I'm older than you, Imani."

"Wow, you're two years older than me."

"Just do what I said, smart-ass."

"I don't have to listen to you. I stay gone because I hate it here. Aaliyah is dead, Elijah is gone, and Mama's always drunk. All she does is drink and cry. I wish I didn't have to live here."

"I don't like being here sometimes either."

"And you get to leave whenever you want, and that's not fair."

"Life isn't fair, Imani."

"Just shut the fuck up, Ayesha, and leave me alone!"

I then slapped Imani, and we started fighting in the living room. She then started pulling my hair, and I pulled hers, yanking her weave ponytail out. The fight continued until Auntie Angie came upstairs to break it up.

"Stop it! Both of you! I'm too damn old to be running up here and breaking up fights!"

"She started it! She hit me first!"

"Imani, go to your room and go to bed! I'm about sick of you," Auntie Angie replied.

Imani yelled, "You always take her side! You treat her better than me! I hate living here!"

"I will come in that room and give you an old-fashioned ass-whupping if you slam another door in this house!"

"I don't know what's gotten into her," I said to Auntie Angie.

"The devil is what's gotten into her. That child is on my nerves. Simone better get her before I do."

Simone stumbled into the living room and said, "What's all that yelling?"

"Ayesha and Imani got into a fight," Auntie Angie said.

"Who won?"

"What do you mean, who won? Simone, ain't nothing funny. You need to get it together and get this house back in order. I'm praying for you," Auntie Angie said.

"The last time I prayed, I asked God to save my daughter, and he ignored me, so I don't need any prayers from you," Simone replied.

"That's that liquor talking. That liquor is the devil. God will make a way. You will get through this. He wouldn't put more on you than you can bear."

"Auntie, where was God when my baby got shot? Where was God when I begged him to save her? Where was God when my baby took her last breath? Is this the same God who let my daughter die but let the niggas who shot her live? What God do you serve?"

"I serve a good God."

"You Christians kill me. God doesn't let shit like this happen. God is supposed to protect people, especially children. My baby was only six, and God let a bullet rip through her body and take her life. I watched my baby choke on her blood! I listened to a fucking doctor tell me there was nothing else he can do! God can't help me if he can't bring my baby back," Simone cried.

"You can't put this all on God. You let the devil in this house. I tried to warn you," Auntie Angie said.

"Are you saying this is all my fault?"

"Simone, I'm not saying that. I'm saying if you wanna blame someone, blame the devil."

"I don't wanna hear this shit right now."

"The truth hurts," Auntie Angie replied.

"Whatever, I'm going to bed," Simone said as she walked away.

"Let's go back downstairs," Auntie Angie said.

Simone was somewhat secretive about her life. I learned a lot about her from Auntie Angie.

"Simone wasn't this bad when Slick died. Slick was all Simone had after Lorraine died. Lorraine was beautiful, and my brother was crazy about her. She was good to him; she couldn't get off that dope. Slick and Lorraine used to shoot up heroin together. Slick kicked it, but Lorraine couldn't stop, and it killed her. Slick was at work when Simone found Lorraine dead with a needle still in her arm in the bathroom. Simone was about Aaliyah's age when that happened. That had to be hard for Simone. Slick used to spoil Simone rotten. That's why she goes after men for money. Her daddy gave her everything, so she expects men to do the same. Tony and Simone never loved each other. They were just two kids who had a baby together."

"I'm not sure if Simone ever really loved Eric. Eric was a good man who gave her security, but the one man she truly loved was Imani's daddy, Darnell. You might not remember much about Darnell because he died when you were four, but that was Simone's only true love. Simone was in love with Darnell, and he was quite handsome, but he lived that life that got him killed. They were engaged to be married. Darnell getting killed was another rough time for Simone. Simone didn't love Damien the way she loved Darnell, and Damien damn sure didn't love her. It was lust, and Damien gave her money, fancy clothes, and anything she desired, but she paid the price for it. That's what the devil does. The devil tricks you by giving you things, but there's always a price for it. Unfortunately, the cost was Aaliyah's life. That's what happens when you dance and make deals with the devil. Aaliyah getting killed added more pain to Simone's life. Simone is damaged. It will take some time, but God will help her heal; I know he will."

My mother bore the heavy burden of grief, a weight accumulated over a lifetime of sorrow and anguish. The memory of discovering her mother's lifeless body, a victim of a heroin overdose, lingers persistently, an ever-present specter refusing to fade. The sudden and violent loss of her fiancé in 1993 inflicted wounds that time could not mend, scars that reopen with each passing year. Then came the slow agony of witnessing her beloved father's battle with lung cancer in 2000, leaving an irreplaceable void in her heart. Yet, perhaps the cruelest blow was the senseless loss of my little sister in a drive-by shooting, a tragedy that shattered her world and plunged her into a sea of despair. Now, as she navigates the turbulent waters of grief once more, her spirit crushed beneath the weight of sorrow, she seeks solace in the numbing embrace of alcohol, attempting to escape the relentless grip of loss. Despite the darkness threatening to engulf her, a faint glimmer of hope remains—a fragile beacon of light, promising healing and redemption if only she can summon the strength to grasp it.

CHAPTER 11

The Devil Stays Busy

September had arrived, and school started the day after Labor Day. When I returned to school, I felt like I was a celebrity being questioned by the paparazzi. Both students and teachers told me they were sorry for my loss, while other students kept asking me what happened and were trying to be nosey. About five students came up to me and told me they heard that Elijah got shot as well, and he died at the hospital. By the grace of God, a bullet never touched Elijah, and I don't know who started that terrible rumor.

"Yo, I'm sorry for what happened to Aaliyah," Malik said.

"Whatever," I replied as I slammed my locker.

"I know we didn't end on good terms, but I am sorry. Aaliyah didn't deserve that."

"Malik, I don't give a fuck how sorry you are. My little sister is dead, and nothing can change that. Just leave me alone."

When I was on my way to class, I heard a student say to another, "The news said that her little sister's daddy was selling dope, and that's why they got killed."

Dame wasn't even Aaliyah's dad. I was so annoyed that I walked right out of school. I was sick of people gossiping, staring, whispering, spreading false information, and asking me questions. I couldn't take it anymore and decided to leave.

TJ stood outside and said, "What up doe? You wanna skip?"

"I would rather be anywhere but here," I replied.

"Let's go to my crib," TJ said.

"Okay, let's go. People are getting on my fucking nerves."

When we got to TJ's house, we sat on the couch, and TJ said, "What happened to Aaliyah is fucked up. I hope the police catch the niggas who did that shit."

"Tell me about it. Even if the police do catch the niggas, it won't bring her back."

"It won't, but at least you'll get some justice. Hit this shit. It'll make you feel better," TJ said as he handed me the blunt.

I took a few hits from the blunt. I started coughing, but after passing it back and forth with TJ, I got the hang of smoking without coughing. Before I knew it, I was high as hell.

"Shit, I'm high as fuck," I chuckled.

"You look high as fuck," TJ replied.

Things got awkward when TJ kissed me.

"TJ, what the fuck? You're my best friend's boyfriend!"

"Me and Kierra ain't even together," TJ said as he attempted to kiss me again.

"That's still my best friend, TJ!"

"Then why are you here?"

"I came over to skip school, that's it. I would never betray my best friend by fucking around with her ex! That's girl code. How could you do this to Kierra? You got her pregnant, and now you're trying to fuck her best friend!"

"Pregnant?"

"Don't play dumb with me, TJ! You gave her the money for the abortion!"

"Yo, you sound crazy as fuck. What abortion? Kierra never told me she was pregnant, and I never gave her money for an abortion. I'm lost here."

"She was seven weeks pregnant when she got an abortion last month. She told me that you gave her the money to pay for the abortion."

"I don't know why Kierra told you that. It couldn't have been my baby. I ain't fucked Kierra in months. She started acting funny, stopped giving me pussy, and she broke up with me before school was out. I didn't know she was pregnant."

"Why would she lie to me?"

"Kierra's on some bullshit. These hoes stay lying."

"Don't call her a ho."

"Kierra is a little ho, and I'm telling Dollar Bill. It makes sense now. She broke up with me to fuck with another nigga. Who knows who her baby daddy is or was?"

"You're such a cornball, TJ. I'm going home. I'm not going back to school today. I'll tell my mom that I'm not feeling well."

I took the bus home, and Simone was passed out on the couch asleep when I got there. I went into my bedroom and cried. It had been the first time I had been in my bed since before Aaliyah's death. I was filled with so much emotion. Today was the day that Aaliyah was supposed to start second grade. She was so excited. Auntie Angie told me not to question God, but I couldn't understand why he would allow an innocent six-year-old to lose her life like that. I fell asleep and dreamed that I was babysitting Imani, Elijah, and Aaliyah and fussing at them about cleaning the house. I would give anything to have those moments with my siblings together again.

"Esha, wake up! Kierra is here," Imani said.

I asked Imani as she changed out of her school uniform, "Do you have homework?"

"No," Imani replied with an attitude.

"Can you please be home on time? Auntie Angie wants you home by six. It's a school night."

"Six? That's some bullshit."

"Do what Auntie Angie says, Imani."

"And if I don't?"

"Imani, don't make this harder than it has to be."

"Blah, blah, blah… shut up talking to me," Imani replied before she left.

"Girl, I'm so tired of that little girl and her smart-ass mouth. She's thirteen going on thirty," I said to Kierra.

"Why the fuck did you tell TJ about the abortion?"

"Excuse me? You're the one who told me that he gave you the money for the abortion, so I assumed that he knew about the pregnancy."

"Why the fuck were you at TJ's house anyway?"

"Because I was tired of people questioning me about what happened to Aaliyah. We skipped to his house, and TJ kissed me. I told him that you were my best friend, and I couldn't do that to you. Why did you lie to me, Kierra?"

"Because it wasn't TJ's baby!"

"If TJ wasn't the father, who was?"

"Dame! You know the truth! Are you happy now?"

"What the fuck, Kierra? Are you fucking serious? That was my mom's boyfriend! When was this going on?"

"I started fucking around with Dame in late May. I didn't tell you because I knew you would judge me. How could I tell you that I was fucking around with Simone's boyfriend? Dame told me to keep everything on the low, and I did. He used to give me money. When I told him that I was pregnant, he gave me the money for the abortion and told me to get rid of it. I couldn't tell anyone who the real father was."

"This is too much. I knew that nigga wasn't shit. He sold drugs, cheated on my mom, got my little sister killed, and he was a child rapist."

"Dame didn't rape me. He never forced me to do anything. I agreed with everything we did with each other. I'm just as guilty."

"That's bullshit, Kierra! Dame was almost thirty! You're fifteen and technically a child. That's statutory rape. He would be in jail for that shit."

"That's why I didn't wanna say anything. You're so judgemental, Ayesha."

"It's not right, Kierra."

"It's not, but Dame looked out for me. My dad is dead, my brother's in college, and my mama works hard but still struggles from time to time."

"I get it. Times get rough, and although it seemed like Dame was doing good deeds, he wasn't. He was manipulating and preying on you, Kierra."

Unfortunately, grown men messing around with underage girls was not uncommon. I knew of men who had sex with teenage girls, almost young enough to be their daughters. They were predators who preyed on minors. It is absolutely despicable and utterly reprehensible for any adult, whether male or female, to engage in any form of sexual content with a minor. Let me make this abundantly clear: there is NO justification, NO excuse, and NO circumstance where this behavior is acceptable. It's not just wrong; it's vile, repulsive, and downright criminal. Minors are vulnerable, impressionable, and unable to consent fully to such acts due to their age and level of maturity. Adults who exploit this vulnerability for their sick gratification deserve nothing but the harshest condemnation and the full weight of the law coming down on them. There is no room for leniency or understanding when it comes to this heinous violation of trust and innocence. Any adult who even entertains the idea of engaging in such despicable behavior should be met with nothing but swift and severe consequences. Protecting children from predators must be an absolute priority, and we must stand united in vehemently denouncing and eradicating this scourge from our society. I found it to be sickening and sad.

Dame was just another sick pedophile, taking advantage of a young, naïve, and impressionable girl. It didn't matter how attractive Kierra was. Kierra was still fifteen, and there was no excuse for a grown man to be having sex with a minor. I had no remorse for Dame. Auntie Angie was right about him being the devil.

When I went downstairs to see Auntie Angie, she was sitting in her living room with Talisha.

"Talisha, what are you doing here?"

"Dawn has been missing for almost a week," Auntie Angie replied to me.

"What?"

"The last time I saw her, she left for work. I haven't seen her since. She's not answering her phone. She wouldn't leave me at home this long unless something bad happened," Talisha said.

"I told Talisha that she could stay the night. Ayesha, I need to speak to you in the kitchen," Auntie Angie said.

"This is so messed up," I said.

"She can stay one, maybe two nights, and if Dawn hasn't returned home, I'm calling Child Protective Services. Charlene is out there getting high, and I have a feeling that something terrible has happened to Dawn. I told that girl what would happen to her when she raised a hand to her mama," Auntie Angie said.

"Auntie, don't say that, and please don't call CPS."

"Ayesha, that girl can't live in that house alone."

"I got an idea. Talisha can stay with us. Elijah is staying with Eric now, and Talisha can sleep in his room."

"Look here, child. You don't pay any bills in this house or buy any groceries to decide that. Simone has had her hands full with you and Imani. She wouldn't know what to do with a fast-tail girl like that."

"Talisha is not that bad."

"Please. That girl dresses like a hussy, wearing those short skirts and belly tops. She'll be pregnant before you know it. Dawn hasn't been the best role model. You know how Dawn was. That girl was loose. She was dancing naked for money, screwing different men, and I heard she was messing around with her landlord. Her landlord goes to Everlasting Grace. He's a married man, old enough to be her daddy. Ain't no telling what she's gotten herself into. I'll warm up some food for that girl, but she can only stay for two nights at the most. Go and keep her company," Auntie Angie replied.

"It feels good to have you here. It reminds me of old times when we had sleepovers upstairs."

Talisha replied, "Those were the good days. It was me, you, Kierra, and Imani. Simone would buy us pizza and a whole bunch of junk food, and she would let us stay up all night. Remember when Simone caught us watching a nasty movie, and we all got whupped?"

"I remember. Imani snitched on us because she wanted to watch cartoons. That's a whupping I'll never forget," I said.

"Remember when we used to pretend we were in a singing group, and I used to fight with Kierra over being the lead singer?"

"Girl, Kierra wanted to be the lead singer so bad," I replied.

"I wanted to live with you. I hated going home. I wouldn't feel anything if my mama died. She would be a dead crackhead to me, and I wouldn't shed a tear or miss her. I would rather it be her than Dawn. Dawn is the reason why I'm not in a foster home. She always took care of me," Talisha said.

"Do you have any idea of where Dawn might be? Does she have a boyfriend? If so, maybe she's at his house," I said.

Talisha replied, "I wouldn't call him her boyfriend; he's more like a trick. I can't remember his name. Dawn said that he started acting jealous, weird, crazy, and then he started threatening her. She didn't take it seriously or go to the police. She just joked about it."

"I'm quite sure that Dawn is okay."

"This isn't like Dawn, Ayesha. I know my sister. I think she's dead," Talisha cried.

"Knock on wood, Talisha. Everything will be okay."

The devil stays busy. Three days later, authorities discovered Dawn's body in an abandoned house located on the East Side. Tragically, she had fallen victim to a fatal gunshot wound, the grim result of jealous, violent actions. The perpetrator eventually surrendered to the police, providing them with the critical information needed to locate Dawn's body. Consequently, Talisha was taken by CPS. She had been through so much within only fifteen years of life. I prayed that Talisha would end up in a nice and cozy home where she felt safe and happy.

CHAPTER 12

Sisters

"Ayesha, this is really unlike you. Your grades have dropped tremendously, and you have multiple absences. If you continue like this next semester, you'll have to retake these classes and make the credits up in summer school. Summer school is one hundred dollars per class," Ms. Hill said.

I can't lie. The first half of the semester of my tenth-grade year was not good. I had a hard time focusing, barely wanted to go to school, and was mentally exhausted from everything that had been going on at home. I was sitting in Ms. Hill's office at school, and she was concerned.

"I'm here to help you. Please give me suggestions on how I can help you improve. You're a very good student with so much potential. I know things have been difficult at home. Would you like to talk about that?"

"Excuse the language, but shit has been fucked up since my sister died. I don't know who my mom is anymore. She kept the house clean, we never missed a meal, and she kept us together as a family. The last time she cooked a meal was before my sister died. She never used to drink this much. I mean, she would smoke blunts at times, but as far as being a fucking alcoholic, she was never like this. My mom takes a drink when she wakes up, she drinks before bedtime, and it's like she gave up on being a mother. My little brother stays with his dad now; my sister is driving me crazy and won't listen. I do the cooking and the cleaning, and when it's time for me to do homework, I'm tired. I didn't sign up for any of this shit."

"I want you to know that I understand the pain your mom is going through. It's something that hits close to home for me. See, I had a baby who didn't make it into this world alive. My child was born stillborn. When I was married to my ex-husband, we had been trying to have a baby for a while, and when we finally found out I was pregnant, it was like a dream come true. We were expecting a baby boy, and my ex-husband was so involved. He even planned the baby shower, which was something I'd never seen before. We put so much love into preparing for our son's arrival. The nursery was decked out with all the trimmings, and everything seemed fine during the pregnancy. That's why it was such a shock when our baby didn't cry when he was born. That moment when I realized something was wrong is one I'll never forget. Coming home to a nursery that was supposed to be filled with the sounds of a baby but was instead silent and empty is an indescribable feeling. Losing a child before they even get a chance to take their first breath is incredibly painful. It's a different kind of pain to have had that child in your arms, to have loved them and cared for them, and then to lose them. I can't even begin to imagine what your mom is going through right now. Ayesha, I want you to know that it's okay to talk about it and feel whatever you're feeling. If you ever need someone to listen, I'm here for you."

"What should I do?"

"I think your mom could benefit from talking to someone who specializes in helping people with grief, like a counselor. If you have any adults you're close to, it might be a good idea to talk to them about finding some help for your mom, like counseling or support groups. Sometimes, talking with someone spiritual, like a pastor or someone from your church, can also be comforting. Depression is tough. It makes you feel really sad and hopeless, and you might not feel like doing much at all. Sometimes, people try to cope by sleeping a lot, drinking, or doing other things that aren't good for them. Losing someone you love is hard, and it takes time to feel better. Your mom's going through a lot, but she still has to be there for you and your siblings. You're young, and it's not your job to take care of everyone like a mom would. Your sister might not be here physically, but she's watching over you like an angel. You can honor her by doing your best and making your mom proud. Maybe try to focus on school, get those grades up, and keep pushing forward. I believe you can do it, Ayesha. As a matter of fact, I know you can do it. If you ever need to talk, my door is always open. Okay, you better head to class now. It would be best if you weren't late. Take care."

To make matters worse, Imani was out of control. She wouldn't listen; she would talk back, kept getting suspended from school, and stayed out past curfew. Simone was hardly sober, and Imani took advantage of that by doing what she wanted to do. It had gotten to the point where Imani started sneaking out of the house with her friends. Imani was beautiful, a little darker than me, and had the most beautiful brown skin, looking like a mixture of Simone and Darnell. She was so talented and had an incredible singing voice. We were inseparable as little kids, but as we got older, we started bickering over things like borrowing clothes and sharing the bathroom. Imani's attitude started getting worse around twelve, and she was often angry, though nobody knew why. Even at her thirteenth birthday party, she didn't seem happy like you'd expect. I figured it was just hormones causing the mood swings.

Simone yelled in the living room as Imani slammed our bedroom door, "It should've been you instead of Aaliyah, you fucking dyke! Don't slam my fucking door!"

I walked in from school and asked, "What is going on?"

Simone replied, "I caught Imani and her friend kissing! Ain't none of that gay shit in my house! And that nasty-ass girl can't come back over here! I don't even want Imani hanging with her!"

I walked into our room and said, "Imani…"

"Leave me alone," Imani said as she cried with her face buried in the pillow.

"You can talk to me," I said.

Imani screamed at the top of her lungs and threw a pillow at me, "Leave me alone! Get out!"

I went back into the living room with Simone. A few minutes later, Imani came storming out towards the door when Simone blocked her and yelled, "You done lost your mothafucking mind! You ain't leaving this house!"

"Move!" Imani yelled.

"Get fucked up if you want to, Imani! Take your ass back in that room," Simone demanded.

Before I knew it, Imani pushed Simone to the floor and stormed out.

"Imani!" I yelled.

"That little bitch done lost her mind," Simone said as she got off the floor.

"Ma, are you okay?"

"That little bitch can't stay here, she gotta go!"

"Ma, she's only thirteen."

"I don't give a fuck! She put her hands on me! Today is Aaliyah's seventh birthday. I woke up this morning mad at myself for forgetting to order Aaliyah a birthday cake, but then it hit me. I didn't order a cake because Aaliyah is fucking dead! I cried so hard. The last thing I needed to see was Imani kissing some bitch! She didn't get that dyke-ass shit from me!"

The streetlights came on, and Imani hadn't arrived home. We weren't too worried then because we thought Imani was just being rebellious. When the clock went past midnight, we started to worry. Hours went by, and Imani was still missing. A few hours turned into twenty-four hours. We contacted the police and searched the neighborhood, but no one saw or heard from Imani. Twenty-four hours turned into forty-eight hours, and everyone was worried sick.

"I'ma beat Imani's ass! It's been two days!" Simone yelled.

"That child needs Jesus! She had no business doing that filthy stuff," Auntie Angie said.

"We don't have no fags and dykes in this family," Simone said.

"Ain't that the truth? However, you were wrong for wishing death on that girl. That wasn't kind, Simone. What if Imani is dead? Are you prepared for the police to tell you that they've found a body? Are you prepared to identify Imani's body at the morgue? Look at what happened to Charlene's daughter! That girl was murdered, and the body was found decomposing! Are you prepared to bury another child, Simone?"

"Auntie, no! Imani pissed me off so bad. It was Aaliyah's birthday; I was upset and said some things I shouldn't have said. I didn't mean it. I'm just so sick of Imani," Simone cried.

"Simone, you gave Slick hell, and God blessed you with girls to give you hell back," Auntie Angie chuckled.

"Ain't nothing funny," Simone replied.

"Someone's at the door," I said.

"Simone, go drink some coffee," Auntie Angie said.

I followed Auntie Angie to her door. When she opened it, Imani was standing on the porch when Auntie Angie said, "Well, well, well, look who's here. Where have you been?"

"I was at my friend's house," Imani replied.

"Why should I let you back in this house?"

"Because I ain't got nowhere to go, and I'm just a kid."

"You weren't just a kid when you were told not to leave this house. Simone was worried sick."

"I don't know why," Imani replied.

"Simone would die if something happened to you, Imani. She didn't mean that. There are girls out here getting raped, pimped out, and killed. I should tear your behind up; I really should. You even had me worried. Your mother's in the house, sitting in my kitchen. Go inside, and the next time you raise a hand to your mother, I'm putting you in the grave."

"I'ma fuck you up!" Simone yelled at Imani.

"Don't touch her, Simone. Both of you sit down. Y'all ain't tearing up my house. Imani, you are long overdue for an ass-whupping, and you know it. Simone, you don't wish death on people, especially on your child. Baby, I know you didn't mean it, but you have to be careful of what you wish for. I know you miss Aaliyah, but you must let her rest. She's watching over you now. You have three other children who need you. That liquor ain't doing you no good. Imani will be in a casket at the rate she's going. This child is already engaging in sinful, filthy acts. Imani, God will send you straight to hell, for it is an abomination," Auntie Angie said.

"Imani, where were you? We were worried," I said to Imani that evening.

"I was at Lanique's house. After Mama caught us kissing, she told Lanique that she couldn't come over anymore. Mama put me on punishment for a month for running away. I was only gone for two days." Imani replied.

"Did Lanique pressure you to kiss her?"

"No."

"Then why were you kissing Lanique?"

"I don't feel like talking about it, Ayesha. Just leave me alone," Imani replied.

"I'll leave you alone. I'm glad that you came home. I don't want anything to happen to you, Imani. You're the only sister that I have left."

Having a younger sister who was acting rebellious and navigating challenges with her sexuality was challenging. Simone and Auntie Angie weren't understanding at all. Simone thought that it was just a phase, and Auntie Angie thought that taking Imani to church, getting her baptized, and forcing her to read Bible scriptures would change her. If I could turn back the hands of time, I would've worked this situation with more empathy, understanding, and a sense of responsibility. Open and non-judgmental communication should've been a priority. Suppose I wanted to establish a strong, supportive relationship with Imani. In that case, it's important to make her feel safe and comfortable enough to confide in and listen to her concerns and feelings without immediately trying to give advice or reprimand. It was my job to guide Imani toward making responsible choices by setting a positive example. Sisters should share the importance of self-respect, self-esteem, and maintaining boundaries in relationships. I was also determined to encourage healthy friendships and interests outside of potentially negative influences that can help redirect Imani's attitude and energy.

To anyone who is facing a similar experience, I would recommend creating a safe space where they feel comfortable discussing their feelings without fear of criticism. Listen actively without imposing your own beliefs or solutions. Offer reassurance that their feelings are valid and normal, and remind them that they don't have to label themselves. Please encourage them to explore resources like LGBTQ+ support groups, books, or online communities where they can find understanding and guidance. Finally, emphasize your unconditional love and support, letting them know you're with them every step of the way.

CHAPTER 13

Senior Year

Let's fast forward to my senior year of high school.

I had a boyfriend named Chase Elliott. We had known each other since elementary school and got together in the eleventh grade. He was cute, light-skinned, tall, went to Cass Tech High School, and lived on LaSalle Boulevard. Chase was a real sweetheart and would always say sweet things and surprise me with small gifts such as candy, teddy bears, cards, and flowers. His parents liked me a lot, and Simone, Auntie Angie, my siblings, Tony, and Eric all liked Chase because he was kind, smart, well-mannered, got good grades, and was far from a street nigga. Auntie Angie just knew that we would get married one day. Our relationship was great until our senior year of high school. I took Ms. Hill's advice, got my grades up, and made it back on the honor roll. I got accepted into multiple colleges, including Central State University in Ohio, but I had no plans of going to a four-year college. That's when my relationship with Chase took a turn.

"You should stay a bit longer. We can go another round," Chase said after we had sex at his house.

"So that we can get caught? Your parents would flip the fuck out if they caught us in the act," I replied.

"Can you believe we're seniors now? Time went by so fast. Have you decided about going to Central State?" Chase asked.

"No."

"Why not?"

"Chase, Central State is about three hours away, and I don't have any family in Ohio. I'm not sure if I want to live alone that far away. It's not an easy decision for me to make."

"You won't be alone; you'll be with me. Ayesha, you got accepted into an HBCU. You're the first in your family. If you're worried about paying for college, they offer financial aid, and you can apply for scholarships."

"It has nothing to do with paying for college. Can you walk me home? We'll talk about this some other time."

"Okay. I'll go grab my jacket," Chase replied.

When I arrived home, Tony's truck was parked in front of my house.

"Daddy, I didn't know you were coming over," I said when I walked into the house.

"I'm here because Simone asked me to come so she can start a fight with me," Tony said as he sat on the sofa and glared at Simone.

"That's not true, Ayesha. I called him over here to talk to him because I need help. Tony, this is Ayesha's senior year. Senior dues, graduation pictures, prom; all that shit costs, and it ain't cheap. I'm just asking for help."

"I told you I'll do what I can."

"You always say that, and you don't do shit. Do you think you did something all because you bought Ayesha a few fucking outfits from Rainbow? That shit can't compare to what I've done for the past seventeen years. It's funny how you claim you don't ever have any money, but you keep a pair of fresh shoes on. Must be nice."

"Money is tight for me right now."

"Have you ever thought that money is tight for me? All you've ever done was make sorry-ass excuses. Hell, I can't get child support from you because you dodge paying that by working under the table. I'm working my ass off to make sure that Ayesha has what she needs, and I need you to step up."

"You know my situation. There ain't much I can do right now."

"Ain't nothing changed about you. That's the last time I will ever ask you to help me out again. You don't have to worry about me asking you for shit else. Get outta my house, Tony. My daughter is good without you."

"Simone, chill out."

"Don't tell me to chill out, Tony. Just get out."

"Esha, I'll call you tomorrow," Tony said before he left.

After Tony left, I said to Simone, "Well, that went left. How was work?"

"I'm so sick of that fucking job, Ayesha. It's only because of the pay and the benefits that I didn't quit. I worked my ass off today."

"Ma, you don't have to worry. We'll be fine."

"I'm not worried at all. It's not about money. I just wanted you to have a better relationship with Tony. I'm tired of that nigga breaking promises and disappointing you. You don't deserve to be treated like that. How can a man expect other men to treat his daughter right, and he treats his daughter like shit? How hypocritical is that? Slick was a damn good daddy. I wanted you to have the great relationship that I had with my daddy with yours, but Tony ain't shit like Slick, that's for damn sure."

Simone was now a customer service representative of Red Star Health Plan of Michigan, Michigan's largest health insurance company. With Tony being inconsistent, Imani's dad being dead, and no extra help from Eric since Elijah lived with him, Simone carried the load of our expenses, which wasn't easy. She worked overtime and did hair on the side to care for us and manage the bills. I made money doing hair so that I could help, even though Simone refused to take money from me and wanted me to focus more on school.

I can't talk about my senior year of high school without mentioning the drama. A crowd gathered in the hallway as a fight broke out at school. Kierra was fighting another student named Quanita Harrison. Quanita was TJ's girlfriend and baby mama, who had given birth to their daughter months prior. TJ had dropped out of school and no longer attended Central. I had no clue why Kierra and Quanita were fighting in the first place.

A male student yelled into the crowd, "World Star!"

Kierra and Quanita continued throwing blows. A school security guard broke up the fight and yelled, "Break it up! Everyone get to class, or else you'll be suspended with Miss Johnson and Miss Harrison!"

"Please tell me you didn't get suspended, Kierra," I said as we left school.

"They suspended me for three days, but it was worth it. I beat Quanita's mothafucking ass," Kierra laughed.

"This is our senior year. You can't afford to get suspended."

"Fuck that bitch. She's just mad because I was fucking TJ while she was pregnant."

"Are you fucking serious?"

"Serious as fuck. That nigga felt guilty about it and finally decided to tell her. She ran up to me and tried to check me, and that's when we started bucking."

"Kierra, why the fuck do you have to be so fucking messy? You don't even want TJ; you just don't want Quanita to have him. You knew he had a girlfriend. Why would you do that?"

"I did it to get back at that bitch. She shouldn't have fucked my ex-boyfriend."

"You and Quanita weren't even friends. You had a few classes with her, that's it."

"I don't give a fuck."

"You should give a fuck. You made a fool of yourself fighting over a nigga. You're one of the prettiest girls at Central. The Kierra I know don't fight over niggas; the niggas fight over her."

"I wasn't fighting over TJ. That bitch wanted to fight me, and I just defended myself."

"Can you blame her? You did fuck her boyfriend while she was pregnant."

"I don't owe her an explanation. I'm not her nigga. Don't check me, check him."

"Kierra, I can't deal with you."

Days later, tragic news circulated through the hallways.

"Kierra, what's wrong? Why are you crying?"

"TJ got killed on Saturday night. He tried to break into a man's house, and the man shot TJ in the fucking face with a shotgun! When his family identified his body, they said what was left of TJ's face looked so bad that the funeral would have to be a closed-casket service. I told TJ to get his GED, get a job, and leave the streets alone. He didn't listen, and now he's dead," Kierra cried.

TJ had dropped out of school in the eleventh grade. Once he dropped out, his mother put him out. From there, TJ lived the rest of the days of his life carjacking and taking cars to chop shops, committing robberies, and home invasions. TJ was always a silly, sometimes annoying, but cool guy. It was sad that he lost his life at eighteen years old. I talked Kierra out of not attending TJ's funeral due to the drama between her and Quanita.

During TJ's repass, Quanita sat at a table by herself, wearing a white T-shirt with TJ's picture on it, and she was holding a baby girl. I walked up to Quanita and asked, "Is this Samiyah?"

"Yeah," Quanita replied.

"She's beautiful."

"Thanks."

"Nita, I haven't had the chance to tell you this, but I'm sorry for your loss. TJ was my friend, and he loved Samiyah," I said.

"I know. TJ loved being a dad."

"Believe it or not, Kierra is sorry as well."

"Ayesha, I ain't never had a problem with you, but I don't care that Kierra is sorry. My last argument with TJ was over Kierra. My baby daddy is dead, and we never got the chance to resolve our problems before he died. TJ won't be here when Samiyah turns one, starts school, and goes to prom and college. If I could talk to him for one last time, I would tell him I love him. I don't wanna do this on my own. Samiyah needs her daddy," Quanita cried.

My heart went out to Quanita as she navigated the difficult path of teenage motherhood, compounded by the tragic loss of her baby's father. The weight of this burden must have felt overwhelming at times as she grappled with the responsibility of raising her daughter without the support and presence of TJ. At that moment, my thoughts turned to Quanita and Samiyah, hoping they find solace and strength amidst their grief. Despite the challenges ahead, I had faith that Quanita's resilience and love for her daughter would guide her through this tough journey, and I silently prayed for their well-being.

"My son is gone! Jesus, help me!" TJ's mother cried.

"That was me when Aaliyah died. I feel her pain. It ain't easy burying a child, especially when it's the only child you have," Simone said as she stared at TJ's mom sobbing.

"I haven't seen you since before I graduated," Malik walked up to me and said.

"Hey, Malik. How are you?" I replied as I hugged him.

"Other than losing my favorite cousin, I'm alright, I guess."

"I'm so sorry for your loss. I know how close you were to TJ, and I hate that we had to see each other on this occasion."

"I know. TJ was never cut out to be in the streets. I had plans to come back and get him once I made it big. Maybe if I hadn't left, he would still be alive," Malik replied.

"Malik, you can't blame yourself for that. That was a choice he made, and unfortunately, it got him killed. May he rest peacefully. On a brighter note, you seem to be kicking ass, playing college basketball in Lansing. A lot of people are predicting that you're going to be the next basketball superstar."

"I hope so. What about you? Are you still with Chase?"

"Yeah, but…"

"But what?" Malik asked.

"Things are a bit complicated. We have different plans after graduation, and it's causing problems between us."

"I got a girl in Lansing, but it ain't nothing serious. I'm more focused on myself and going pro. If you want my advice, do what's best for you," Malik said before walking off.

Chase had been pressuring me for months about going to Central State. I had decided not to go. Although Chase was highly disappointed, we agreed to have a long-distance relationship, but I had a change of heart on my prom night. After we finished dancing to the song *Take Money To Make Money* by Stretch Money, I told Chase, "I need to talk to you. Can we go outside for a moment?"

"Sure," Chase replied.

"Chase, I had a nice time with you tonight. I hate to ruin this night by telling you this."

"Telling me what?"

"I know we agreed to stay together when you go to college this fall, but who are we kidding? You'll be in another state around many college girls, and I'll be here, waiting on your phone call, hoping there's not another girl in your dorm."

"Come with me, Ayesha."

"Chase, we talked about this. I can't."

"I can't believe you'd rather become a hairstylist than go to college."

"You sound like Auntie Angie."

"She's right. You're wasting your life away, Ayesha. I understand that you have a passion for doing hair, but why not at least go to college, get a business degree, and use your degree to start your business in the future?"

"Because I don't need a damn business degree to start a business, and I don't want to move to Ohio, Chase. That's what you want. That's not what I want. I don't want to go to nursing school, I don't want to go to college to get a business degree, and I don't want to retire from nursing as my great-aunt did. Life is too short, and I plan to live it by doing something that I love and making it into a business."

"Get to the point, Ayesha. What's the real reason you brought me out here?"

"Chase, I think we should go our separate ways."

"Wow. I can't believe you're breaking up with me on prom night. I missed my prom to take you to your prom, and I'm getting dumped. Unbelievable."

"I love you, Chase. If it's meant to be, we'll be together again."

Chase yelled before storming back into prom, "Fuck you, Ayesha!"

Prom night was the end of my relationship with Chase.

"I still can't believe you let that boy get away," Auntie Angie said as we prepared to head to my high school graduation.

"Not this again. I made my decision. Can we drop this?"

"Auntie, she's only eighteen. She's too young to be thinking about marriage. Let her live her life," Simone replied.

"What do you know? You got pregnant in high school, had babies with different men out of wedlock, and didn't go to college. You didn't do much to make Slick proud when he was alive. You want her to ruin her life like you ruined yours."

"That's what you think? My daughter is graduating from Central High School, class of two thousand seven, with honors, and she made it through high school without getting pregnant. She's one of the top students at her school. She has a dream of doing something big. What's wrong with that? What's wrong with starting a business? Ayesha ain't no dummy, and she'll be fine. She'll be successful one day, watch. Ayesha is the reason why my life is far from ruined. She's the reason why my daddy is proud of me, and he's smiling down on me. I did something right with her. I wanted to drink myself to death and die when Aaliyah died, but God is good. God gave me the strength I needed to get myself together for my children. Maybe I didn't do much to make my daddy proud when he was alive, but I guarantee you he's proud of me now," Simone replied. "Let's go, Ayesha. I don't want you to be late for the ceremony," Simone said as she glared at Auntie Angie.

That weekend, Simone threw a backyard barbecue to celebrate my graduation. Among the attendees were Kierra, friends from school and our neighborhood, Elijah, Eric and Tanya, Tony, and a handful of family members.

"Girl, what the fuck is he doing here? Did you invite him?" Kierra asked, pointing at Chase.

"Yes. Chase told me that he wanted to talk. It's not like we're getting back together. Can you believe this nigga fucked someone else on prom night?"

"What? I mean, you did break up with him at prom. That was cold as fuck, Ayesha."

"Kierra, he had sex with his ex-girlfriend."

"Ouch! Is this the same ex-girlfriend who goes to Cass with Chase?"

"Yes. Her name is Kendra, and she hates my guts. Chase swore that he no longer had feelings for her. I guess he wanted to make me jealous. They can have each other."

Chase walked up to us and asked Kierra, "Can you give me a minute to talk to Ayesha?"

"Talk to her for what, Chase?"

"Kierra, please give us a minute," I said.

"I brought you something," Chase said as he handed me a teddy bear that wore a graduation cap.

"He's a cute little bear. Thanks."

"I just wanted to apologize. I shouldn't have had sex with Kendra that night. That was not cool. We ended our relationship on a bad note."

"Chase, it's okay. I broke up with you that night. We weren't together."

"If there was any chance of us getting back together, I guess I screwed that up. Anyway, I love you; I mean, I wish you the best. Congratulations, Ayesha," Chase said as he placed a kiss on my cheek.

After Chase left, Auntie Angie said, "That's a fine young man. You're making a big mistake."

CHAPTER 14

Red Flags

"Keep this house clean. I don't want any wild-ass parties, no niggas running in and outta here, and no pregnancies. I'm too young to be somebody's grandma," Simone said.

"You ain't that young," Imani mumbled.

"What did you say, Imani?" Simone asked.

"Nothing," Imani replied.

"I know y'all love to hit them clubs, but please come home at a decent time," Simone said.

"Ma, the clubs don't close until two, and the clubs don't start slapping until midnight," I replied.

"I don't care. I don't need you worrying Auntie Angie to death. You know how she is, and she will be keeping an eye on you and calling me if you get outta line," Simone replied.

"I'm twenty-one, and Imani is nineteen. We're both adults, but you're treating us like kids by giving us rules."

"If I don't lay down any rules, you'll do what you wanna do and turn this house upside down. There's more to adulthood than partying and doing what you want. Being grown comes with being responsible, paying bills, buying groceries, budgeting, having self-control, and making wise decisions. You might end up making some tough choices, like canceling a nail appointment because you have to use that money to pay the DTE bill, or not being able to buy them new Jordans because you have to buy groceries. Buying fast food every day won't help you, and it's a quick way to go broke. Y'all need to create a grocery budget."

"We're responsible enough to live on our own and can handle this," I replied.

"I still have a key, and you never know when I'll pop up," Simone said. "Oh, and I better see both of you in church," Simone continued.

"Is that it?" Imani asked.

"I could stay a little bit longer, smart-ass. You ain't too grown to get popped," Simone said to Imani.

"I love you. Call me when you get home," I said to Simone.

In 2010, Simone married Keith Watkins. She moved to Southfield with him, leaving Imani and me in our duplex. Keith owned a used car dealership in Detroit called 313 Motor Sales. He had a nine-year-old daughter named Kennedy from a previous relationship. Keith was a handsome, charming, classy, and relaxed guy who made Simone very happy. Seeing my mom find love and joy filled me with happiness as well. When she became closer to God and surrendered her life to God, everything in her life seemed to fall into place.

"Thank God, she's gone. Mama can be irritating as fuck at times," Imani said.

"At least we got the crib to ourselves," I replied.

"I feel you. I'll be performing at Harpos tonight. Make sure to tell Kierra to come with you, and maybe you'll find a new boo tonight," Imani said.

At twenty-one, I was feeling on top of the world. I had a job and a car of my own, and I was finally living independently. No one could tell me anything! After finishing high school, I went to P&A Scholars and got my cosmetology license. I was slaying as a hairstylist, but it wasn't all sunshine and rainbows. I had my fair share of drama in the salon world, dealing with shady owners and catty coworkers. I relied heavily on social media to attract clients. Posting my work online helped me build a dope portfolio showing off my skills and style. It wasn't just about getting new clients; social media let me connect with my regulars in a cool, personal way, but as my online presence grew, so did the haters. Some of the stylists in the salon got jealous of the attention I was getting online. It turned the place into a real mess. Let me tell you, working in some of those salons was pure ghetto, and the dating scene wasn't any different.

It had been three years since I broke up with Chase and graduated from Central High School. Chase had met a girl while attending Central State. The two got married, and Chase decided to reside in Ohio permanently. Chase hit me up on social media, and we exchanged numbers. It was nice catching up at first, but things got awkward fast.

"Hello?"

"What are you wearing?" Chase asked over the phone.

"Shouldn't you be asking your wife that?"

"Come on, Ayesha. Tell me what you're wearing."

"Chase, you're being weird right now."

"Are you wearing a bra? I want you to rub your nipples for me," Chase said as he masturbated during the call.

"I'm not having phone sex with you. Goodbye, Chase."

On top of that, Chase started sending me sexual texts and dick pics and even talked about coming to Detroit to hook up. I ended up blocking his number and blocked him from my social media. Chase had me fucked up because I don't mess with married men. I couldn't help but feel sorry for his wife.

"I can't believe you got me on the mothafucking Eastside," Kierra said while we were at Harpos.

"You don't say that when we go to Belle Isle. That's considered the Eastside, and we're here to support Imani," I replied.

A handsome guy walked up to me and said, "Excuse me, sweetheart. You're so beautiful, and I can't help but introduce myself. Eastside Bankroll is my rap name, but you can call me Darius."

The caramel-colored guy named Darius stood about five-foot-nine, wearing a black tee, black jeans, a black Detroit snapback, black and white Nike Air Force Ones, chains around his neck, a nice watch on his wrist, and tattoos on his body. I was rocking a cute tan dress, gold heels, and gold jewelry. I had my hair in a sew-in with a side bang and beautiful long body waves. I was intrigued by Darius and found him quite attractive.

"I'm Ayesha. It's nice to meet you, Darius."

"How old are you?" Darius asked.

"I'm twenty-one."

"You just a baby," Darius replied.

"A baby with a job, car, and her own crib," I replied.

"Damn, straight? Okay, I see you, Miss Independent," Darius said.

"How old are you?" I asked.

"I'm twenty-four."

"You're only three years older than me, but you called me a baby."

"I was just fucking around. I got jokes for days, and I just wanted to make you smile. What side of town are you from? I haven't seen you around here."

"I'm from the Westside," I replied.

"Oh, you a Westside girl? No wonder," Darius said.

"What's that supposed to mean?"

"It means that some of the finest women in the city are from the Westside. We have plenty of fine and thick women on this side of town, but none like you. I would love to get to know you, Miss Ayesha."

"Let me give you my number. It's three-one-three, six-one-nine, zero-eight-zero-seven," I said as Darius pulled out his phone.

"I'll be hitting you up," Darius replied.

"Some of the finest women may be from the Westside, but clearly, the finest fellas are from the Eastside. I'll see you around, handsome," I said to Darius before I walked away.

"Bitch, I see you. Ol' boy is cute and all, but he's not tall enough for me," Kierra said.

"Girl, he's the right height for me. He might be bigger in other places, if you know what I mean," I said.

"True," Kierra said.

"You killed that performance at Harpos tonight, Imani. I'm so proud of you," I said to Imani.

"Did I perform better than Eastside Bankroll? I saw you talking to him tonight," Imani replied.

"And? I'm single," I said.

"That nigga ain't shit, Ayesha."

"How do you know, Imani?"

"My auntie used to manage him. He's a ho. He'll fuck anybody, he has a baby mama, and I heard that he beat up his baby mama. Plus, that nigga ain't got it like that. These niggas always rap about shit they don't have. Please don't waste any time or energy on him. Well, a bitch is tired; I'm going to bed. Goodnight," Imani said.

"I hope you made it home safe. Sweet dreams, beautiful," a text from Darius said.

"I did. Goodnight, handsome," I replied.

Darius sent me texts every day, and when he wasn't in the studio recording, he would call, and we would talk on the phone for hours. He would only call me during late hours. I didn't think anything of it at the time. We learned a lot about each other. Darius told me that his mother was on crack when he was a child, he was in different foster homes, he'd been to jail for a drug charge, and like my father, his father was a deadbeat. He told me that writing rhymes and rapping helped him through a lot and stay out of jail.

Darius asked me on our date at Capers Steakhouse, "Have you ever been here before?"

"No, this is my first time here," I replied.

"This place got the best steaks in the city. Order whatever you want, baby."

"Good, I'm starving. A T-bone sounds good right about now," I replied.

"I have something to tell you. I have a daughter. Her name is Nylah, and she's five. I love my baby to death, but her mama is too much drama. I don't know if telling you this changes the vibe between us, but I'm really feeling you, Ayesha."

"Darius, I'm glad that you told me, and it doesn't change a thing. I like kids. Maybe I'll meet her one day."

"You had me nervous for a second. I can't take not being able to see that pretty face again," Darius said.

When we were done eating, the waitress handed Darius the bill, and Darius handed the waitress his debit card. The waitress returned and said, "The card was declined."

"Can you try again?" Darius replied.

"It declined again. Do you have any other payment method?"

"I don't understand why it declined. It's money on my card," Darius replied to the waitress.

"I got it," I said as I grabbed my purse and handed cash to the waitress.

"I can't let you do that," Darius said.

"Don't worry about it," I replied.

"This is so embarrassing. I'm sorry. It's the first of the month. I just bought my daughter some shoes, and I gotta make this up to you somehow."

"It's okay. Shit happens. I had a great time with you tonight," I said.

When I arrived home, Imani asked, "How was your first date with Bankroll?"

"It went okay," I replied.

"What happened?"

"His card was declined at the restaurant. The bill was over a hundred dollars, and I paid it. It was worth every penny because that food was fire. Sis, if you want a good steak, the Eastside is where you gotta go," I replied.

"I told you. That nigga tricked you into paying the bill. He knew he didn't have the money, and you fell for it. He's such a bum and broke-ass nigga. You can do better."

"Imani, it's the first of the month, and he has a daughter he takes care of."

"Whose car did he pick you up in? That nigga's always driving somebody else's car or sitting in the passenger seat."

"We rode in his car."

"His car? Is this the same car that's always in the shop? Believe that shit if you want to," Imani said.

Darius and I continued to date. We had a lot of great sex. He lived on the Eastside near Skateland. He was roommates with his uncle, but I had never been to his house. We would always have sex at my house, a motel, or in his car. Darius used to bring me to his studio sessions. I was at his shows when he performed, and he had me in one of his rap videos. When he was short on cash for studio time, I covered the rest. It seemed like I was covering a lot.

"I hope I'm not too late," Darius said when he arrived at the salon with his daughter.

"You're not too late, babe," I said as I kissed him. I then said to his daughter, "You must be Nylah. Are you ready for your makeover, Princess Nylah?"

"Yes," Nylah replied.

"It won't be long. I'll call you when I'm done with Nylah's hair," I told Darius.

Darius brought Nylah to her hair appointment thirty minutes late. Although Nylah was a sweet girl, she had a hard time staying still; she kept whining, and the press-n-curl hairstyle I gave her took longer than it was supposed to. When I called Darius to pick up Nylah from the shop, he wouldn't answer his phone.

"Girl, I don't know where he is. I was done with his daughter's hair over three hours ago. He won't answer his phone. I just got done with my last client. I'm the only stylist who's still here, and I'm closing the shop. I did this little girl's hair, fed her, bought her McDonald's, but I didn't sign up to be a fucking nanny. I don't know where to take this little girl," I said to Kierra on the phone.

"Take her to the house with you; have him pick her up from there, stepmom," Kierra suggested.

"Bitch, you got jokes," I replied.

"That's why I don't fuck with niggas with kids," Kierra said.

"I'll call you back. I need to call Darius again," I replied.

Ten minutes later, Darius walks into the salon, eyes bloodshot red, smelling like weed and liquor. I had been blowing his phone up, and this nigga was out smoking and drinking while I was babysitting his daughter. I was so irritated.

"Darius, where have you been? I've been calling you and texting you for hours."

"I'm sorry. I lost track of time. You hooked Nylah up. Did she give you any problems?"

"No, she was fine," I replied.

"Fuck…"

"What's wrong?"

"I don't have the money to pay you for Nylah's hair. I left my wallet at home," Darius replied.

"Don't worry. It's on me."

"That's why I love you. You always have my back. I'll slide through after I drop Nylah off," Darius said before he left the salon with Nylah.

Darius showed up at my place with scratches on him, looking like he had been in an altercation. He told me that he and his baby mama had gotten into an argument, and she attacked him. We spent the night at my house, getting drunk off Cîroc and having sex.

"Why are you calling me? We live in the same house, Imani."

"Because I don't wanna walk in on you and Darius, but I called to tell you that Mama just pulled up."

"What? It's eight in the morning! What the fuck is she doing here this early? She didn't call, give a heads-up, or anything!"

"She's coming upstairs. I would get dressed if I were you," Imani replied.

"Why is there a pizza box, a Cîroc bottle, and weed on the table? This house is a mess. Look at these dishes in the sink. I raised y'all better than this. Clean this house up," Simone ranted.

"Mama, it ain't even that bad in here," Imani said to Simone.

"Hey," I said.

Simone replied, "Did y'all have a party or something? Get this house cleaned up, and why does it smell like some nigga been up in here?"

Darius walked out of my bedroom, wearing a wife-beater and basketball shorts, saying, "Ayesha, y'all got some cereal, eggs, bacon, or something? A nigga hungry as fuck. I should be getting breakfast in bed after dicking you down last night."

"Who are you?" Simone asked Darius.

"Ma, this is my boyfriend, Darius," I replied.

"It's nice to meet you, Miss Jones. I really love your daughter," Darius said as he put his arms around my waist.

"Is that so?" Simone replied.

"Yeah, and I'm thinking about marrying her one day."

"Hell naw," Imani chuckled.

"Darius, you haven't known my daughter for that long. How could you be so sure about this?"

"When I first met Ayesha, it was love at first sight."

"Where did you meet my daughter?"

"At Harpos," Imani replied.

"At one of those rap shows?" Simone asked.

"Yeah," Darius replied.

Simone asked, "What do you do for a living?"

"I'm a rapper. I just got done working on my new mixtape."

"Let me rephrase that, Darius. What is your full-time job?"

"Spitting rhymes is my full-time job," Darius replied.

"Lord have mercy," Simone mumbled.

Imani busted out laughing, and I said, "Girl, be quiet."

"Darius, can you give me a few minutes to talk to my daughters?"

"Fasho, Miss Jones. I'm getting ready to grab my stuff and head to the crib," Darius replied.

"That's a good idea, Darius, and it's Missus Watkins," Simone told Darius.

After Darius left, Simone said, "How the hell do you have a broke-ass boyfriend named Bankroll? That's false advertising. He's unemployed, donates plasma to buy weed, has you paying for dates, has you babysitting his daughter, only calls you at night, and beats on his baby mama. I don't like this nigga at all."

"Imani, why did you tell her that?"

"Did I lie?" Imani replied to me.

"Baby, you can do better," Simone said.

"Mama, I tried to tell her," Imani said to Simone.

"First of all, Darius is always busy recording. He doesn't beat on his baby mama; she's always attacking him, and he's struggling with finding a job because he has a felony. We all make mistakes; people change, and you, of all people, should know that," I told Simone.

"Have you been to his house yet?" Simone questioned.

"No, and that's because his uncle is funny-acting."

"That boy is one hell of a liar. Ayesha, you are way smarter than this. You see the red flags; you know this boy ain't worth a damn. If he's hitting on his baby mama, he'll put his hands on you, and if he does, I'll send his ass right to the funeral home. I'm saved, but I don't play about my kids," Simone said.

One night, we drove to the Bullfrog Bar & Grill for Darius's show. Darius told me that his car was in the shop, and I decided to drive us in my car. When we arrived, Darius's baby mama got out of the same Pontiac G6 that Darius drove, which was supposedly in the shop. When she confronted Darius in the parking lot, I felt like I was on an episode of *Cheaters*. His baby mama was very pretty, with brown skin like Imani, black hair, and slanted eyes.

Brandi said to me, "You must be Ayesha. I found your business card in *my* car. I don't know you, and you don't know me, but I'm his baby mama. This nigga stays in *my* house, that car is in *my* name, and I pay the note. I didn't come here to fight you; I just thought you should know. You can have him," Brandi said.

"Man, shut the fuck up and take your ass home!" Darius yelled.

"Your shit will be on the curb when you get home. Go stay with her," Brandi said.

"Don't touch my shit, Brandi! I'm not fucking playing!"

"Mothafucka, I paid for everything you got! I'm working overtime to pay the bills, take care of Nylah, and you don't help me with shit! All you do is lie, cheat, smoke, drink, and spit those wack-ass raps!" Brandi replied to Darius.

While Darius and Brandi had their dispute, a big, tall, handsome guy with hazel eyes said to me, "That nigga Eastside Bankroll is a bitch. He won't hit any nigga but will beat up his baby mama. I almost had to fuck that nigga up because he tried to get tough with me. That nigga tried to battle me, and I murdered his garbage-ass on the mic. Baby girl, you don't need no ho-ass nigga like that."

I got in my car and drove off. I cried the whole ride home, feeling heartbroken, embarrassed, and dumb as hell. Simone and Imani tried to warn me. I broke it off with Darius; he kept calling and texting, and I kept ignoring him. He popped up at my house one day, and we talked in whoever's car he drove. It wasn't Brandi's car this time.

"Me and my baby mama ain't together; we just live together," Darius said.

"It doesn't matter now," I said.

"Ayesha, we can work this out. I'm done with Brandi. We can stay here, live together, I'll get custody of Nylah, we can get married, and have a baby," Darius replied.

"Not interested."

"Can you at least loan me eighty dollars? Brandi put me out, and I need money to get a room," Darius replied.

"That ain't got shit to do with me," I said as I opened the car door.

"Fuck outta my car then, bitch," Darius said as he pushed me out of the car and sped off.

I yelled, "You fucking bastard!"

When Darius pushed me out of the car, I fell onto the concrete and hurt myself, scraping my knee and elbow. All it took was one time for a nigga to think he could ever put his hands on me. He pushed me, and a push will turn into a punch one day. I changed my number and blocked him from my social media. A month later, Brandi contacted me to tell me that Darius was locked up. He was arrested for domestic violence and charges related to theft and robbery.

Brandi said to me on the phone, "I had been with Darius for seven years, and we were still together when he was fucking you. When Darius went to jail, I stayed loyal, and I held him down. I held that nigga down when he had nothing, bought his clothes when he came home from jail, and he still fucked other bitches and drove my car to cheat. Darius cheated on me so many times that I lost count, and he has other kids that he doesn't claim. He had the nerve to put his hands on me every time I called him on his bullshit. He used to tell me that he loved my natural hair because it was long, and my hair was the first thing he pulled every time we fought. When I stayed with Darius's mama, his raggedy-ass mama watched him put his hands on me. She never defended me and condoned all her son's bullshit. As a woman, how can you allow your son to treat another woman that way?"

"My friends told me so many times to leave him, but I didn't wanna raise my daughter in a single-parent household. That was an excuse that I used to stay in that fucked-up relationship. Darius has slapped me, punched me, choked me, kicked me, pulled a gun on me, called me bitches, hoes, sluts, and every name but a child of God. I thought he would kill me this time, but he killed the baby that was inside of me. I was pregnant with our second child and lost the baby because he lost control of his fists. The sound of Nylah's cries made him remove his hands from around my neck. Darius was mad at me for putting him out and changing the locks on the door. The neighbors called the police, and I'm surprised the police came this time. I lost my unborn, but I didn't lose my life. I'm happy that I'm still here for Nylah. Nylah was the best gift he'd ever given me. Other than that, all I got was lies, disrespect, beatings, bruises, and pain. I don't care if I ever see Darius again."

Hearing Brandi's story made me realize how much I dodged a bullet. Her story made me look back on Simone and Dame's relationship. Dame never hit me or my other siblings, but if Simone had told the truth about the fights between them, CPS would've placed us in foster care. Never ignore the red flags. Ignoring red flags in a relationship, especially those associated with toxic behavior and domestic violence, can have bad consequences. Dismissing such warning signs may lead to escalating violence, and the person who resorts to destructive behavior might eventually direct it toward their partner. It's important to recognize these red flags early on and take them seriously. Engaging in a relationship with someone prone to violent outbursts poses a significant risk to one's physical and emotional well-being. Domestic violence can affect anyone regardless of gender, and it is important to recognize that both women and men can be victims or perpetrators in such relationships. The societal stereotype often depicts domestic violence as a problem exclusively faced by women, but men can also find themselves in abusive situations. Support services and resources are available to assist both women and men facing domestic violence. Organizations like the National Domestic Violence Hotline (1-800-799-SAFE) and local shelters provide confidential assistance, counseling, and resources to help survivors break free from abusive relationships.

CHAPTER 15

Fairytale

"Whatever happened to your bae?" My client asked at the salon.

"You're talking about Darius. Camille, I kicked that nigga to the curb. That's been done and over with," I replied.

"Aww, y'all were a cute couple. Why did you break up with him? He was always up here bringing you lunch and stuff," Camille said.

"He was bringing me lunch that I was paying for, and coming up here to borrow money that he never paid back. Darius was a loser. I had to let him go. Girl, he was still in a relationship with his baby mama; they still lived together, and he was driving her car that we had sex in."

"Really?"

"Yes, and he was abusive. His baby mama had a miscarriage because of him. He's locked up now, thank God."

"What a scrub!"

"He's in the past now. Life is too short to be in a miserable relationship," I replied.

"Well, Malik is single," Camille said.

"Camille, why are you telling me this?"

"Because you're single now."

"I dated your little brother in high school. We were young, and it's been four or five years since I saw him. I'm not a groupie or gold digger."

"I know you're not a gold digger. You were with a broke guy for months, and that shows you don't go after guys for their money. I don't want my brother to get some random whore pregnant and owe nearly half of his hard-earned salary to her for child support. He needs someone to settle down with. My brother needs someone like you," Camille said.

"If you say so, Camille."

I remember when Kierra and I went out to eat at Starter's Bar and Grill to celebrate her birthday and her getting into nursing school. Starter's was her favorite restaurant, so I thought I would do something special for her by treating her to dinner. We hadn't linked up in a while.

"Congratulations on getting into nursing school. My girl is about to be an RN, and I don't mean a real nigga; I mean a registered nurse! Oh, and Happy Birthday," I said as we made a toast before sipping our drinks.

"Thank you. I'm tired of working as a CNA. I'm overworked and underpaid. Nurses get paid good money, and I need it," Kierra replied.

"I knew you would get in. You were always smart, just fast as hell," I chuckled.

"Fuck you. I was not fast," Kierra chuckled.

"Girl, bye."

"Bitch, you probably fucked more niggas than me!"

"I have not," I replied.

"You fucked Malik, Chase, Darius, and probably way more than that," Kierra said.

"For the record, I can still count my total number of guys on one hand. You're dating two guys at the same time right now," I replied.

"I'm dating two, not fucking two. I just don't take these niggas seriously. All these niggas do is lie and cheat. Look at Chase. That nigga got a whole wife but still tried to fuck you. Plus, most of these niggas got kids and baby mama drama. Don't get me started on Darius. I don't want kids, and I damn sure don't want anyone else's kids. Until a nigga put a ring on it, I'ma do me," Kierra said.

"I haven't told you this, but Malik contacted me."

"Are you fucking serious? How did you get in contact with him?" Kierra replied.

"You know that his sister is one of my regular clients. She gave Malik my number without permission."

"Permission? Bitch, Malik is a fucking basketball star now! Why the fuck does she need permission?"

"I asked about Malik a few times, but I didn't tell her to give him my number. I'm not some fucking groupie, Kierra."

"Girl, you're overthinking this whole situation. If a basketball player hits my line, I'm riding his dick that night. Call me a groupie all you want. What happened next?"

"Malik called me, and we went out on a date. He sent his driver to pick me up from my house, and I met him at Saltwater Prime."

"Saltwater Prime? Isn't that the expensive seafood restaurant in Troy?"

"Yes. Malik loves that place; it's his favorite restaurant. He rented out the whole restaurant for just us two. The date went well."

"And?"

"Kierra, I know where you're going with this."

"Malik is rich, famous, and fine as hell. You don't know how fucking lucky you are."

"He's a famous basketball player. You know that many basketball players have notorious reputations for being hoes. He's probably fucking all kinds of celebrities and beautiful models when he's on the road. He could have anybody."

"You're right; he could have anybody, but Malik is not showing interest in anybody; he's showing interest in you. He took the time to contact you. Obviously, there's something special about you. Stop talking like you're not fucking gorgeous with a banging-ass body. Ayesha, you can pull any nigga you want."

"Kierra, I'm not trying to get hurt. If Malik played me once, what makes you think he won't do it again? He had me looking stupid in high school, and I'll be damned if I look stupid again, especially on television."

"You can't hold that against him. That was in high school. Niggas in high school be young, dumb, and full of cum. He deserves another chance. See where things go. Shit, I would rather get cheated on by a rich nigga than a broke nigga. You could hook me up with one of his teammates. What I wanna know is did you fuck him?" Kierra said.

"No! We've only been on one date!"

"Ayesha, why does that matter when you gave him some pussy when you were fifteen? Girl, my back would've been blown out by now."

Malik had become a famous professional basketball player and played for the Detroit Spark Plugs. He was a star athlete at Central High School and in college, and he was drafted into the basketball league in 2008. I started dating Malik in late 2011. I didn't have any intentions of becoming the girlfriend of a basketball player. I didn't have the desire to be followed by cameras all the time or see my name on any gossip sites, and I damn sure wasn't willing to take a chance of being publicly humiliated. I also had trust issues because of what happened in my previous relationship with Darius, another reason I had my guard up. Malik was persistent and reassured me that he wasn't Darius, so I gave in. Most women would brag about being the girlfriend of someone famous, but I didn't. I kept everything low-key. I still worked as a hairstylist, and no one at the salon knew who my boyfriend was. I didn't post anything about my relationship with Malik on social media, and even when I would attend his games, I didn't give any indication to the public that I was his girlfriend. I didn't want anyone in my business.

Malik's basketball career kept him busy, and we couldn't spend as much time as I wanted. In 2012, he had a game scheduled for Valentine's Day in New York. I was a little disappointed because I wanted to spend Valentine's Day with him, but I understood who he was and his busy lifestyle. I thought I would spend Valentine's Day alone, watching Malik on television, but to my surprise, Malik flew me on a private charter plane to New York. It was the first time I had flown on a plane. I attended his game in New York, and we went out to eat. Then, we returned to his hotel suite. The high-rise penthouse suite overlooked New York City and was decorated with candles, pink and red flowers, and pink and red balloons. As slow jams played in the background, he gifted me with a beautiful diamond bracelet that he purchased from MJ Diamonds and a mink jacket that he purchased from Dittrich Furs.

After I bathed, I stood in the suite, dressed in a sexy black lace bra with matching panties. I was getting ready to fuck the sexiest man alive. Malik stood in the suite, rocking his black briefs, showing off his lean and muscular body that reached six foot six. And let me tell you, those waves in his hair were still on point! His chest and arms were inked up, adding to his allure and driving me wild. I've always had a thing for guys with tattoos. I couldn't help but check out the bulge in his briefs as his dick started to stand at attention.

Malik whispered in my ear as he kissed my neck and nibbled on my earlobe, "Let me make love to you."

Malik then picked me up and gently laid me on the bed, kissing my neck, sucking on my breasts, and licking and kissing my stomach. He then gently took my panties off with his teeth, kissed and licked my thighs, and buried his face between my legs while rubbing my nipples, giving me the best head I'd ever had in my life.

"I'm cumming," I moaned as Malik licked and sucked on my clit.

His beard was dripping and soaked with my juices. I sucked my juices off his dick, and I could feel my pussy getting wetter as I devoured his delicious milk chocolate. I was giving head like a professional porn star. Malik placed my legs over his shoulders, sliding his thickness inside my wetness, giving me deep, slow strokes of passion as I scratched his back, moaning and enjoying every stroke. He then made me get on all fours, kissing and sucking on both of my ass cheeks, sliding his tongue up and down my crack before thrusting me in the doggy-style position as I clenched the sheets. Malik's dick felt amazing. It felt nothing like the first time. There was no pain. Malik was not the same selfish sixteen-year-old boy who just wanted to bust and get a nut. He was a grown man, more mature and passionate. He wanted to please me and had his mouth on every part of my body that night. His strokes of passion weren't too fast or too slow, and he wasn't too rough. We ended the night with me riding his dick, both cumming at the same time. We made love in multiple positions, and I had multiple orgasms that night. It was a night of passion in New York.

Simone and Keith would have us come to their house on the first Sunday of every month for dinner. Malik had a game in Los Angeles, so it was just me, Elijah, and Kennedy that Sunday. Imani hadn't been coming over. When asked, I would say that Imani had a show or studio session, but the truth was that Imani didn't want to be there.

"Ayesha, I haven't seen you at church lately," Simone said as she finished cooking.

"I've been busy."

"Are you too busy to come worship and give God praise, or too busy at the clubs with Kierra or spending time with Malik?"

"Ma, Imani hasn't been coming to church either. What about her?"

"Imani ain't here, and she's a different story. That girl is a piece of work. Where is my future son-in-law?"

"He's in Los Angeles."

"That's right. Malik is playing against Los Angeles tomorrow night," Simone replied.

"You called him your future son-in-law. How can you be so sure that Malik is going to marry me?"

"You moved in with him, so I'm assuming you're getting married, or do you plan on shacking up forever, Ayesha?"

"We've been together for a little over a year now. Marriage takes time. I'm not rushing anything."

"If he can move you into his fancy high-rise downtown, he can put a ring on it."

After we ate Simone's delicious fried chicken, macaroni and cheese, collard greens, and cornbread muffins, Keith asked to speak with me in his home office. Keith and I got along well. He was the biggest Spark Plugs fan, and he liked Malik a lot.

"Tell Malik I can't thank him enough for season passes and box suites to all his games. Your mother told me that you moved in with him."

"I did."

"Do you enjoy living in downtown Detroit?"

"Minus the traffic, I like living downtown. My mom feels we should be married since we're living together now. Some couples wait two, five, and ten years before getting married."

"That's true, and I believe there's nothing wrong with living together before getting married," Keith replied.

"You agree with me, right?"

"I agree, but it doesn't take a man years to know if he wants you to be his wife. It doesn't take us very long at all. A man knows whether he wants you to be his wife, girlfriend, side chick, or friend with benefits. When Robyn had Kennedy, we lived together, and she kept talking about marriage. I would always tell her that I wanted to be more financially secure. In reality, I wasn't so sure about marrying her. I'm not saying that if a man tells a woman he wants to be more financially stable, it's an excuse to dodge marriage. There's nothing wrong with wanting financial stability before tying the knot. Financial difficulties caused many divorces, but that was my way of telling Robyn that I didn't want to marry her. My father told me that if I didn't plan on making Robyn my wife, let her go, and I did. I was with Robyn for ten years and never married her, but it took me less than a year to know that I wanted to spend the rest of my life with Simone."

"I get what you're saying, Keith."

"I like Malik. He's okay with me. As long as he makes you happy, I'm happy."

In 2013, we had a Christmas party on Christmas Eve at our place. It was an intimate gathering of close family and friends. After everyone exchanged gifts, Malik proposed to me.

"Ayesha, these two years, you haven't asked me for anything. I had to beg you to let me buy you a car so you can get rid of your hooptie."

"That hooptie used to be my Auntie Angie's car. It had sentimental value."

"I'm glad that you finally let me upgrade you. That car had a million miles on it. All jokes aside, you're not in this for the money. You love me for me. You don't care about the money or the fame, you don't care to be the center of attention, and you're the same Detroit girl who loves Faygo Red Pop, chili cheese fries, and Better Made Red Hot Barbecue Chips. I did you wrong in high school, but I promised I would never let you go if I got you back. Ayesha Nicole Jones, I want you to become Ayesha Nicole Davis. Will you marry me?" Malik opened the engagement ring box, revealing the beautiful oval-shaped diamond ring.

"Yes, I'll marry you!"

It didn't take us very long to plan our wedding. I became Ayesha Nicole Davis on August 16, 2014. Our beautiful private wedding was an outdoor and indoor event held at the Luxury Hills Banquet Center in Northville. The ceremony was held outside, and the reception was held inside. Pink has always been my favorite color, so our wedding colors were light pink, white, and rose gold. The bridesmaids wore light pink satin dresses, the groomsmen wore black tuxedos and light pink vests, Malik wore a white tuxedo with a light pink vest, and I walked down the aisle in a stunning white strapless trumpet mermaid wedding gown. Kierra was my maid of honor, and Malik's best man was one of his teammates. Tony walked me down the aisle to give me away while Imani sang *You Bring Me Joy* by Anita Baker.

The pastor said, "Dearly beloved family and friends, we gather here today in the presence of love, joy, and hope to celebrate the union of Malik and Ayesha. Today is a day of great significance as we witness the joining of two hearts, two lives, and two souls in the sacred bond of marriage. Let us begin our time together by reading a passage that beautifully encapsulates the essence of marriage. First Corinthians, chapter thirteen, verses four through seven, reminds us that *love is patient and kind. It does not envy, it does not boast, it is not proud. It does not dishonor others, is not self-seeking, is not easily angered, and keeps no record of wrongs. Love does not delight in evil but rejoices with the truth. It always protects, always trusts, always hopes, always perseveres.* Marriage is not merely a legal contract; it is a sacred covenant, a commitment made between two individuals before the eyes of the divine. It is a promise to love and cherish, support and encourage, and stand by each other through thick and thin."

"As we witness the union of Malik and Ayesha today, let us remember that they are entering into a covenant that mirrors the covenant between humanity and the divine. This covenant is built on the foundation of love, the kind of love that the Apostle Paul beautifully describes in Corinthians. In the journey of marriage, you are embarking on a life together filled with the potential for growth, laughter, and shared experiences. The love you share must be patient, kind, and understanding. It must be a love that seeks the well-being of the other, a love that finds joy in each other's successes and supports one another in times of challenge. Marriage is not always easy, but it is through the challenges that your love will be tested and strengthened. Remember that true love is not just a fleeting emotion; it is a deliberate choice, a commitment to continue choosing each other daily."

"As you build the foundation of your marriage, consider the qualities of love mentioned in Corinthians. Be patient with one another, be kind in your words and actions, and let your humility guide your interactions. Celebrate each other's achievements, and in times of difficulty, be each other's refuge and strength. As you stand here today, surrounded by the love and support of your family and friends, may you embark on this beautiful journey of marriage with hearts full of love, minds open to growth, and a commitment to cherish each other through all the seasons of life. May your marriage be a testament to the enduring power of love and inspire those around you to seek and cultivate the same depth of love in their lives. With the blessing of family, friends, and the divine, go forth and build a life together filled with love beyond measure."

My wedding day was beautiful, but the day of my dreams felt more like a nightmare. I was sick the entire day. Five days before the wedding, I found out that I was pregnant. It explained why I felt so nauseous at my wedding. I had gained weight and had to get last-minute alterations to my dress. During the reception, I was in the restroom vomiting when Simone stood outside the stall and said, "I'ma be a grandma. I ain't even fifty yet."

"What are you talking about?" I said as I walked out of the stall to wash my hands.

"Ayesha Nicole, do I look like Boo-Boo the Fool? I had four kids."

"Okay, I'm pregnant. My gynecologist told me at my annual exam. I told Malik, and he's excited. He's hoping for a boy."

"It seems like you're having a girl to me. Girls make you sick. You, Imani, and Aaliyah kept me sick those whole pregnancies."

"Did you see Daddy's girlfriend with him?" I asked Simone.

"I saw her. She's not bad-looking, but she's too young for Tony's ass."

"She's only seven years older than me. That's so weird. Daddy seems to be a better father to the kids he has with her. I can't lie. I'm a bit jealous of his relationship with them," I replied.

"Ayesha, don't waste your energy on that today. Today is your wedding day, a celebration of love and happiness. You just married a king. You're a queen, so wear the crown like you're meant to."

Our honeymoon in Bali was a dream come true. From the moment we landed, the vibrant culture and stunning landscapes swept us away. We spent days lounging on pristine beaches, the turquoise waters lapping gently on our feet as we sipped on fruity virgin cocktails and soaked up the sun. Our taste buds were treated to a symphony of flavors as we sampled the local cuisine, from spicy satay skewers to fragrant rice dishes bursting with tropical fruits and spices. Each meal was a culinary adventure, and we found ourselves lingering over dinners, savoring every bite. One exhilarating highlight of our trip was a helicopter ride over the lush greenery of the island. As we soared high above the treetops, I felt a rush of adrenaline and awe at the breathtaking scenery unfolding below us. It was a moment I will never forget, the thrill of adventure mingling with the beauty of the landscape. But perhaps the most unforgettable aspect of our honeymoon was the intimacy we shared behind closed doors. Our passion was ignited by the exotic surroundings as we indulged in passionate lovemaking, exploring each other's bodies with a sense of intimacy and desire. Each night was a celebration of our love, leaving us both breathless and exhilarated. As we reluctantly bid farewell to Bali and boarded our flight home, we realized that our honeymoon had been everything we had hoped for. It was a time of love, adventure, and unforgettable memories that would stay with us for a lifetime.

After I returned from our honeymoon, I decided to go to Simone's house. When I walked in, Simone asked, "How's married life treating you?"

"It's wonderful. It's everything I can imagine and more. Malik and I are preparing to move into our house. We decided to purchase the house in West Bloomfield. Malik wanted to buy a house near the Manoogian Mansion, but he ended up going with the one I picked instead. I can't wait until you see it. We have a pool and a beautiful view of Pine Lake."

"You'll be closer to me. Southfield to West Bloomfield ain't that far. How was Bali?"

"Ma, Bali was breathtaking."

"I thought my honeymoon in Hawaii was something. I saw the pictures you posted. You got me wanting to visit Bali."

"I'm really in love with Malik."

"I can tell. You haven't stopped glowing yet. I know the feeling. Keith makes me feel the same way. I haven't felt like this since I was with Darnell. I never had these feelings for Tony. Eric and I were two different people from two different worlds, and Dame was the worst fucking mistake of my life, but Keith is amazing. Plus, he's good in bed. I can't get enough of that man."

"Ma, that is too much information. I did not need to hear that."

"I can't wait until you have my granddaughter."

"Granddaughter? Malik and I are having a boy."

"We'll see when you get that ultrasound. You're carrying a girl."

Simone was right. Our daughter Maliyah Simone Davis was born on February 17, 2015. I named her after Malik and my late sister, combining both names. She was expected to be born on March 30, 2015. I had a difficult pregnancy. I felt sick all the time, had horrible migraines, my blood pressure was all out of whack, and Maliyah was born prematurely. Maliyah had to spend some weeks in the NICU. The arrival of a new baby is often believed to bring about changes in a marriage or relationship. The challenges of caring for a newborn, such as sleepless nights, constant responsibilities, and adjustments in routines, can lead to stress and exhaustion. These factors may contribute to tension in the relationship and have an impact on intimacy and the couple's sex life, but Maliyah's birth strengthened the bond between Malik and me. Having a premature child was immensely frightening and emotionally turbulent for both of us. The sight of our baby connected to medical equipment in the NICU was overwhelming as we grappled with the uncertainty and unpredictability. The emotional rollercoaster of fear, guilt, and sadness was compounded by the separation from Maliyah, who often needed extended medical care. During that time, I would always think about Ms Hill and how she told me that she gave birth to a stillborn. My biggest fear was coming home to a nursery with no baby, as she did.

I took Simone's advice by praying more and worrying less, and God answered my prayers. My princess was a fighter, and I eventually brought her to our big, beautiful new home in West Bloomfield. When Malik wasn't on the road, he was a big help to Maliyah. He never complained, no matter how much she cried.

"I'ma teach her how to hoop," Malik said as he held Maliyah in his arms.

"Who said I wanted our daughter to play basketball? She might do hair like her mommy," I said as we stood in the nursery.

"Speaking of hair, you don't have to be in such a rush to open the salon. I make enough money to take care of you and Maliyah. Besides, I like you being a sexy housewife."

"I didn't sign up to be a sexy housewife. This is my dream. I've been doing hair since I had Barbies and baby dolls. You know how much opening my salon means to me."

"I get it, but don't ever feel like you must work hard. As long as you're my wife, you'll always be well taken care of, and now that you have my child, she'll always be taken care of, regardless of what happens between us. I promise you that," Malik said as he kissed me. "Motherhood looks sexy on you," Malik continued.

"Boy, bye. I don't feel very sexy. I need to get my ass back in the gym."

"I don't see why. I like the baby weight on you. I'm married to the baddest chick in the game. My wife is fine as fuck with a pretty face, small waist, big titties, and a fat ass. You look thicker than cold grits and thick in all the right places. You can still rock a bikini, and niggas' jaws would drop at the sight of you. On God, you look more beautiful than ever. Baby, women are paying thousands of dollars to have the body you have. You got me ready to shoot up the club again and have another baby," Malik said.

"Sir, we're not having any more babies anytime soon. Maliyah is enough for right now."

"We'll see. I don't think you realize how beautiful you were when you were pregnant. You're even more beautiful now," Malik smirked.

"I didn't feel very beautiful when I was pregnant. I felt fat as fuck."

"That's not what I saw. I saw a beautiful pregnant woman whose caramel skin glowed. I saw titties that got bigger, reminding me of juicy melons, giving me the urge to suck on them mothafuckas. I watched your ass get fatter, and I wanted to rub, grab, and smack it every time I got the chance. I remember seeing you waddling with my princess in your big, round, beautiful belly, and how much I admired your thick calves. I can't forget how sweet, juicy, wet, and good that pregnant pussy was," Malik replied.

Malik had a way with words. After I had Maliyah, I had so many insecurities about my body. Malik would always remind me of my beauty and say that I looked even more beautiful with the extra pounds.

My life felt like a fairytale. I was married to my king and living in a palace with our precious princess. We were in the honeymoon phase of our marriage. While he was on the road, he would FaceTime me and tell me how much he missed and loved me. Malik spoiled me and would surprise me with jewelry, cars, and exotic trips, and it didn't have to be Valentine's Day, my birthday, or Christmas for him to do so. He made every day feel like a holiday. We were a Black celebrity power couple, living the glamorous life of the rich and famous, throwing lavish parties at our home in West Bloomfield, spending cold Michigan winters at our condo in Miami, and enjoying summers aboard our yacht on the Detroit River. We graced magazine covers and inspired memes and posts on social media. People looked up to us as relationship role models and admired our bond. We both got tattoos of each other's names: I tattooed his name on the upper right side of my chest, and he tattooed my name on his right forearm. Our sex life was amazing. When I was fully healed after giving birth, it was on and popping. We couldn't keep our hands off each other and would have sex in the morning, afternoon, and evening—in the bedroom, shower, pool, kitchen, car, on vacations, you name it. And that's how I became pregnant with our second child.

CHAPTER 16

Motherhood

"I want to thank you all for coming to the grand opening of D'Goddess Salon and Spa. I want to make a toast to much success," I said as I raised my champagne flute.

In 2018, I experienced one of my life's most significant moments and accomplishments – the grand opening of D'Goddess Salon and Spa. My dream of becoming an entrepreneur had come true. The grand opening event was beautifully decorated by Noteworthy Event Décor and More, who decorated my wedding and baby showers. Noteworthy designed the beautiful pink and rose gold balloon arch displayed at the grand opening. The stylists serviced guests. Refreshments included shrimp cocktails, cold sandwich sliders, fruit and veggie trays, meat and cheese charcuterie boards, sparkling grape juice, bottled water, and champagne. The venue was ideal, boasting ample space, and its location on East Jefferson, just minutes away from Belle Isle, added to its allure. D'Goddess swiftly achieved success, earning top ratings and reviews and establishing a commendable reputation for delivering high-quality professional services. Residents from Detroit, Metro

Detroit, and even celebrities frequented D'Goddess for a range of beauty services, including hairstyling, nail services, makeup, facials, and waxing. While Auntie Angie was more skeptical, thinking I might be wasting my life doing hair, Simone always believed in my dream of owning a salon.

"Mama, I wanna do hair just like you, but I don't wanna do hair in the house. I'm gonna own a hair shop when I grow up," an eight-year-old me said to Simone.

"Baby, let me tell you something real. I believe in you, but you have to believe in yourself. Back when I was your age, I had big dreams just like you. Auntie Angie didn't think much of them and thought I was talking nonsense. I even had a whole name picked out. D'Goddess Hair Salon would've been the name of my salon. But you know what? Things didn't quite work out the way I planned."

"What happened, Mama?"

"Life happened. I got pregnant with you, then Imani, and then Elijah, and now I'm pregnant with another baby. My hands are full, and my dreams are on hold. That's motherhood for you. But that doesn't mean your dreams won't come true. You keep pushing, keep believing, and who knows? Maybe you'll make your dream a reality one day."

After opening the salon that year, I introduced D'Goddess Hair Collection, a website specializing in bundles and wigs, available at www.dgoddesshairco.com. The website also gained immediate success and a reputation for selling quality hair, providing excellent customer service, and offering fast delivery. I put Simone in charge of managing the salon and orders from the website. Before I became a successful Black entrepreneur, I was a stay-at-home mother for three years, and it wasn't always easy.

I gave birth to our second child on May 25, 2016. I named her Milan Chanel Davis, after Milan, Italy, where she was conceived. We had too much fun on that vacation, so much fun that we conceived another baby. I carried her full term, and my pregnancy with her wasn't nearly as complicated as my pregnancy with Maliyah. However, life at home with Milan felt more difficult.

"Babe... Babe, Milan is crying," I said as I woke up and tried to wake Malik.

"Shit," I whispered to myself.

I then got out of bed and headed to the nursery. I grabbed Milan, held her in my arms, and prepared to feed her. Before I knew it, Maliyah started crying. I thought to myself, *"What the fuck was I thinking having another baby while my first one is still in diapers?"*

"Both girls are asleep. Hallelujah, thank you, Jesus," I said as I prepared to make breakfast for Malik in the kitchen.

"How did you sleep last night?"

"Sleep? I barely slept at all. Milan kept crying," I replied.

"Why didn't you wake me up?"

"I tried to wake you. You were knocked out. Having a one-year-old and a three-month-old ain't for the weak. I love our girls, but this is more complicated than I thought."

"Baby, it doesn't have to be complicated, and you know that. We can afford a nanny. It'll make things easier," Malik said as he hugged me from behind and kissed my cheek.

"There's no need for us to do that. I got this."

"You sure?"

"Yes, I'm sure. I could do this if my mom could handle four kids independently."

"You're not doing this alone, Ayesha. You have me," Malik said as he kissed me.

"Where are you going? You don't want any breakfast?"

"I ate some fruit earlier. I'm heading to a meeting with Coach and the rest of the team. I'll be back. Love you. See you soon," Malik said before he left.

"Mmm… right there. Don't stop," I moaned as Malik made love to me that night.

"I have to stop now," Malik said as we were interrupted by a crying Milan.

"Damnit, just when I was about to cum. All this kid does is cry. Maliyah didn't cry this much," I said as I pushed Malik off me and got dressed.

"She's a baby. Babies cry. This dick will still be here when you put Milan back to sleep," Malik said as he smacked me on the ass.

Malik was knocked out when I returned to our bedroom after feeding Milan and putting her back to sleep. I was pissed. I then grabbed my vibrator, gave myself an orgasm, and fell asleep.

"How are my goddaughters?" Kierra asked while we were on the phone.

"They're good, I guess," I replied.

"You guess? What's that supposed to mean?"

"I don't know, Kierra. I love the family Malik and I created, but this isn't easy. I couldn't even finish having sex with Malik last night because Milan started crying. When I first had Maliyah, things were different. I felt different. I was excited about being a new mom. I had more patience, I didn't get as frustrated, and Malik always helped me, but now I feel like a single parent with Milan. At home, he's not very helpful with the girls. I'm the one who's feeding, changing, bathing, and singing lullabies to the girls, while he's on his fucking PlayStation, playing the game in his man cave or shooting pool with the fellas."

"Girl, you're a rich bitch. What the fuck are you complaining about? Just hire a nanny."

"That's what Malik suggested, and I refuse to do that. I'm very protective of my girls. People are weird. What if we hire a nanny, and she tries to kidnap them or some shit? Besides, I can take care of my daughters. I should be the one caring for them, not some stranger. I wouldn't trade Maliyah and Milan for the world. I love them to death, but motherhood can be exhausting sometimes."

"I'm glad I don't have any kids. I'm fine with the two goddaughters I have. Rashad keeps talking about having kids and marriage."

"Rashad seems like a solid guy. Don't be afraid of tying the knot and having kids with him. It's not as scary as it seems, trust me."

"That's easy for you to say. Maliyah and Milan were both born with silver spoons in their mouths. They'll be attending fancy-ass private schools and shit. Rashad and I are both nurses. Our kids won't be struggling, but we won't be able to give our kids the same lifestyle that you give yours."

"As long as I'm the godmother, your kids will be fine, Kierra."

"Girl, I don't want any kids, and I'm unsure if I'll marry Rashad. It's bad enough that we work together at the same damn hospital. He's been talking about moving in together. I see this nigga every day at work, and I'm not ready for us to live together. Our relationship is fine the way it is. I have my apartment; he has his. When I want some dick, I'll spend the night with him, or he'll spend the night with me, but neither one of us won't stay too long. I love my space, privacy, and freedom. That's another reason why I don't want kids."

"Space, privacy, and freedom… boy, how I miss those days," I replied.

"Baby, wake up," Malik said one night while kissing and rubbing on me as I slept.

"Malik, I'm tired. Maybe tomorrow night."

"Ayesha, it's been weeks since we had sex. It's like I practically have to beg you for some pussy, and you always turn me down by telling me that you're too tired or not in the mood. What's up with that?"

"It's the truth, Malik. I'm not in the mood because I'm always tired."

"Then start getting some rest."

"When do I have time to rest? Every time I try to take a nap, one of the girls starts crying. I can't even recall the last time I had proper rest," I replied with an attitude.

"Ayesha, I told you we can hire a nanny. You're the one making shit harder than it has to be."

"I don't want some fucking stranger raising my kids, Malik."

"What do you want, Ayesha? Lately, it seems like all you want is problems."

"What's that supposed to mean, Malik?"

"I don't know what's going on with you, but all you do is walk around with a fucking attitude. It's like you're on the rag every day now."

"Oh, wow. Just because you can't get any pussy tonight, you're in your feelings."

"I'm in my feelings because you're constantly changing moods. One minute you're frustrated, next minute you're sad, next minute you're okay, next minute you're mad at the fucking world, and I don't know what's going on. You haven't been the same since Milan was born. I talked to my mom, and she said you might need to see someone."

"You talked to your mom about me?"

"Baby, I'm just concerned, that's all."

"If you're concerned about me, then talk to me! Don't talk to other people about me, especially your judgmental-ass mother!"

Malik was right about me. I wasn't the same after Milan was born. I was always irritated, stressed, or sad. I would break down and cry at times. I didn't feel like myself. Hell, I didn't even look like myself. I would walk around with my hair in a messy bun, pajamas on all day, with bags underneath my eyes, feeling exhausted and overwhelmed. Milan was a colicky baby and would cry nonstop. I blamed myself, felt like I was doing something wrong, and felt like I was a bad mother when I couldn't get her to stop crying. Sex was out of the question.

My sex drive decreased dramatically. My libido was low, and I had no desire to have sex with Malik. I was not myself.

"I must admit, I had marital counseling before I married my husband, but I've never had counseling for myself other than talking to a school counselor, but that was way back in high school," I said as I sat in the office of Sylvia Prescott.

Sylvia Prescott became my psychologist. Her office was in Southfield. She was a beautiful woman with black locs, beautiful caramel-colored skin like mine, almond-shaped brown eyes, and a small stud earring in her nose. Sylvia had a very down-to-earth attitude, was a good listener, and was easy to talk to.

"That's okay. It's the first time for everything. I'm happy that you reached out. Mental health care has unfortunately been stigmatized within the Black community, creating a pervasive taboo that prevents open discussions and acceptance of mental health issues. Our people need to overcome this stigma and prioritize mental health care. Racism, discrimination, inequalities, stress, and trauma contribute to a lot of mental health issues within our community. Seeking mental health care helps heal and improve your well-being. Well, let's talk. Where would you like to begin, Ayesha?"

"I was recently diagnosed with postpartum depression. I have two daughters, and they're fifteen months apart. My oldest is one, and my youngest was born in May. I feel so bad for saying this, but to get away for a few hours feels good. I love my girls, but I am overwhelmed. I feel as though I have no one to talk to. My husband is dismissive. He was helpful with our first child, but not so much with our second child. He feels that hiring a nanny is the answer to my problems. I'm married to a star. I live in a mansion, I drive luxury vehicles, and my daughters were born with silver spoons in their mouths, but here I am complaining to you about motherhood. You would think that because of my lifestyle, I shouldn't complain. For years, my mother received government assistance, I shared a bedroom with two sisters, and I lived in the hood. My mother was a single parent, but she didn't complain as much as I did. She made it work with what she had and had less than me. I sound like a spoiled brat. How can someone like me have postpartum depression, right?"

"Wrong. You told me you had another child in May, and your daughters are fifteen months apart. You got pregnant again before your oldest daughter could take her first steps. Many women would feel overwhelmed if they were in your shoes. Postpartum depression does not exclusively affect people with low incomes or single mothers. Postpartum is a mental health condition that can impact women regardless of their socioeconomic status, marital status, or any other demographic factor. It can affect women from all walks of life, including those who are financially stable and in stable relationships. Do you know how many mothers I've talked to about postpartum depression? Most are married and economically stable, but money isn't everything. If it were, I wouldn't have millionaires coming into my office, talking about how they're contemplating suicide. Many of my clients are wealthy, but wealth can't fix what's broken inside."

"I feel so ashamed," I cried.

"Ayesha, postpartum depression isn't something to be ashamed of. It is not a choice; it's not something women can snap out of or overcome through willpower alone."

"Sylvia, I don't know what to do."

"I recommend openly communicating your feelings and needs with your husband, family, and friends. Your mother might've made raising four kids by herself look easy, but I'm sure she sometimes felt overwhelmed. Try talking with her. She might give you some wisdom and great motherly advice to guide you. Having a reliable support network can alleviate some of the emotional burden. Maintaining a healthy lifestyle is also important. Regular exercise, a balanced diet, and sufficient sleep contribute to physical and mental well-being. Adequate rest is essential for new mommies, and delegating household tasks can help reduce stress. Try engaging in activities that give you joy and relaxation. Hobbies, self-care, and leisure time can provide a necessary break from the demands of motherhood. Create a structured routine and understand that asking for help is okay. These recommendations should help you through this process. You got this, Ayesha," Sylvia said.

I was blessed to have a mother to help me during my challenging journey through postpartum depression. Simone was a lifesaver in those difficult times and supported me in caring for my daughters. Her presence and assistance not only eased the burden of my struggles but also became a pillar of strength, allowing me to navigate through the complexities of motherhood with a sense of solace and reassurance.

Simone absolutely loves being a grandmother. She's stylish, youthful, sexy, and radiates confidence, so the girls call her *Glamma*. Even though she always says, *"I'm done raising kids,"* she'll flip the fuck out if she doesn't see her granddaughters for too long. Maliyah and Milan got the more chilled-out and saved version of Simone. She doesn't even curse around them. The Simone I grew up with was straight-up hood. Not to mention how much she spoils them! When the girls stay over at her place, I don't even need to pack their clothes because they have a wardrobe and a ton of toys at Simone's house. They get to choose what they want to eat, which was definitely not the case when I was growing up. At her house, the girls can be as wild as they want, doing things that would've definitely gotten me and my siblings in trouble. Simone is in denial and won't admit that she lets Maliyah and Milan get away with murder. But honestly, Simone is the best grandmother a kid could ever have.

"How have you been getting along with Malik's mama?" Simone asked.

"Juanita's okay. She's a bit overbearing and judgmental. I have postpartum depression, and she acts as if I'm an unfit mother."

"Girl, misery loves company. That woman hardly smiles. I wouldn't smile if my husband stayed cheating on me. Did I tell you that her husband tried to make a pass at me?"

"Ma, I'm not surprised. Maurice can't keep his eyes off you, and he's always flirting with you."

"I'm not interested in another woman's husband. What I look like messing around with Malik's daddy? I'm happy with my husband. When I was with Eric, his mama couldn't stand me. That bougie bitch didn't think I was good enough for her son. Tanya went to Mumford with Eric, and things didn't work out when Tanya left Detroit for college, but Eric's mama loved her some Tanya. I know Eric made his mama happy when he married her. At least Elijah likes Tanya, and she's a good mother to him. It wasn't until I became a stepmother that I realized what it's like to love a bonus child as your own. God called Aaliyah home, but when I married Keith, I was blessed with another daughter. Being a mother to Kennedy has been a true blessing. Watching her grow and witnessing her milestones has brought so much joy and meaning to my life."

"I had my issues with Tanya, but I appreciate how she cared for Elijah and helped raise my son into a respectable and fine young man. Tanya stepped up to the plate when I was broken. I was so messed up when Aaliyah got killed. I was drinking every day, depressed, and didn't care what I looked like. Elijah was having nightmares, and I didn't get him help. I was in a dark place and needed to get myself help. It didn't help that I missed the court date, so I didn't make it hard for Eric to get custody. I should've fought harder, but after Aaliyah died, I didn't have any fight left in me. I believe that I had postpartum depression after I had Imani. I was nineteen with my second child. We were living on Burlingame off Linwood."

"Wait a minute. When did we live on Burlingame?" I asked.

"When I got with Darnell, my daddy hated him. He couldn't stand him because Darnell was in the streets. When I got pregnant with Imani, my daddy told me I had to find somewhere else to live. Daddy didn't have to tell me twice. An hour later, Darnell pulled up in his Monte Carlo. I had you with me, and we left. Darnell drove us to the house on Burlingame, told me it was our new home, and took me shopping to buy new furniture. After Imani was born, you were in the terrible twos stage, and you were a handful. I didn't have much help at the house. Darnell was never home and was too busy working in the streets. Not once did my daddy visit me at the house on Burlingame. When Auntie Angie visited, she helped me out a lot with caring for you and Imani, even though she talked a lot of shit. I didn't care because I needed all the help I could get."

"I had my struggles with motherhood. Imagine having three baby daddies; one is dead, the other is a useless-ass deadbeat, and the other is a weekend and holiday daddy. You don't know what having four kids attending three different schools is like. You don't know what it's like not to be able to keep a steady job, not because you're lazy but because your work schedule interferes with your kids' school schedules. These jobs don't wanna hear that you don't have a babysitter. Lucky for me, I made money right from the comfort of my home doing hair. I spent years wiping asses, noses, and tears. Y'all wore me out. I couldn't take a shower, piss, or a nap without one of y'all bugging me for something. I don't regret a thing. I love y'all, and I'm proud of my babies. I feel like I did something right. Have you talked to Tony?" Simone asked.

"I haven't talked to him since he came to see me in the hospital when Milan was born. I saw the pics he posted of the twins' first day of kindergarten. At least he showed up for them on their big day."

"Well, I was there for your first day of kindergarten. That should mean something," Simone said.

"It means more than you know."

When I was younger, I didn't think that I was anything like my mother, but the older I got, I realized I was just like her. When I became a mother, I knew I wanted to be actively involved in my children's lives and be a hands-on mom, just like my mother. I didn't wish to have nannies and personal assistants raising my kids. I wanted to be the one who got my kids ready for school, did their hair, made their meals, helped them with homework, went to PTA meetings, afterschool activities, and recitals, and that's the type of mother I am today. I learned from Simone. She got us ready for school every morning, kept our hair laid, packed lunches, made it to every parent-teacher conference meeting and school concert, chaperoned on school field trips, helped us with homework, kept us fed, cleaned up our messes, and made motherhood look more accessible than it was.

Motherhood isn't easy, but it's one of the best things that ever happened to me. Maliyah and Milan are my worlds. Maliyah and Milan are not just my offspring; they represent the very essence of my world. Their laughter, dreams, and aspirations have become the driving forces behind the decisions I make and the paths I choose to tread. During the chaos and beauty of parenthood, they have served as the catalysts that propelled me to embark on a remarkable journey – the establishment of D'Goddess. D'Goddess is not just a business; it manifests my aspirations, a testament to my dreams for my children, and a legacy I am determined to leave behind. Through this venture, I strive to create a lasting impact for myself and, more importantly, for them. I earnestly desire that they inherit a thriving enterprise and a legacy built on passion, resilience, and unwavering belief. As a mother, my greatest wish is to instill in my daughters the belief that their dreams are attainable. I want them to understand that life is an expansive canvas upon which they can paint their aspirations.

D'Goddess is not just a business endeavor; it is a living example that dreams can be transformed into reality with dedication and a strong belief in oneself.

CHAPTER 17

2020

"Kierra, is the Coronavirus worse than the flu like they say it is?"

"It is. The hospital is overcrowded and understaffed. We have too many patients and don't have enough beds or staff to care for them. We don't have enough PPE equipment, and I'm not getting paid enough money to go through this shit."

"I thought this virus was a hoax at first."

"I wish, but it's not. If it's the end of the world, God should say that. At least I won't have to pay rent," Kierra said.

"Girl, you are something else. I have to call you back. Imani is calling me."

"Kiss my goddaughters for me," Kierra replied.

"Hello?" I answered the other line.

"Did you hear the news?" Imani asked.

"What news?"

"Sexy Stackz is pregnant."

"Who the hell is Sexy Stackz, Imani?"

"Sexy Stackz is a popular stripper, video vixen, and a jump-off in Miami. She has been linked to many high-profile men. I performed at a show in ATL last year, and she was there. I just texted you."

Imani's text was a link to a celebrity gossip website. When I clicked on the link, I saw a picture of a pretty light-skinned chick with black hair and hazel eyes, and Malik was asleep next to her in a bed. The headline read, *"Sexy Stackz Allegedly Pregnant by Spark Plugs Player Malik Davis."*

"Did you get the text?" Imani asked.

"Yeah, I got it."

"It's news everywhere. Everyone's talking about it on gossip sites and social media."

"Everyone's talking about it, but I'm the last to know. I feel so fucking stupid," I replied.

"Is Malik home?"

"No, but he should be walking in the door soon."

"I'm sorry, I had to be the one to tell you."

"You did nothing wrong, Imani. Let me call you back. He just walked in."

"Baby, I can explain," Malik said as he walked in.

I slapped Malik and said, "Explain what? When did you plan on telling me, Malik? Why did I have to find out about this other bitch on the internet?"

"Baby, Amber is lying!"

"Amber? You even know her government name. Are you telling me that this picture on the internet is Photoshopped?"

"No, it's not," Malik replied.

"Where did you meet Amber, Sexy Stackz, or whatever the fuck her name is?"

"She danced at Cedric's bachelor party in Miami. One thing led to another, we fucked that night, but I'm not in love with her. Bitches like her try to pin babies on famous niggas all the time. This shit ain't nothing but a money grab. That baby ain't mine."

"Are you sure about that, Malik? How could you fucking do this to me? I never cheated on you in this marriage! I never questioned you about being with other women on the road! I never checked any phones! I wanted to believe you were faithful, even though my gut always told me something different. I know Amber isn't the first bitch you cheated on me with. Maybe she's the first to claim that she's pregnant by you and expose you for your infidelity, but I'm not stupid, Malik. I'm unsure if I never questioned you about cheating because I already knew or because I didn't want to know. I'm heartbroken and humiliated. You put our lives at risk. What if I caught a disease that couldn't be cured because of your infidelity? You've destroyed this marriage and our family. We are done, and I'm filing for divorce."

"Ayesha, I love you! Don't do this to me!" Malik begged as he tried to hold me.

"Don't fucking touch me!" I screamed and cried.

"Mommy, why are you crying?" Maliyah said as she stood next to Milan.

"Mommy is okay. Let's get ready for bed," I told the girls. "Get the fuck out," I whispered to Malik as I walked away.

"Are you sure about doing this?" Kierra asked as we sat in my family room.

"I'm sure. I've made my decision, Kierra. The thought of him making love to some bitch the way he made love to me sickens me, Kierra."

"Have you spoken to Malik?"

"I haven't spoken to him since last night after I told him to get out. He's been blowing my phone up, calling, sending texts, and begging, but I don't want shit to do with him right now."

"If he's doing all that, then it's obvious he still loves you, Ayesha. Don't be so quick to assume that this bitch is telling the truth. Who's to say that he's the father of her baby? She's a clout-chaser," Kierra said.

"Malik still cheated and embarrassed me. I had to put my phone on DND because people wouldn't stop calling and asking questions. This is exactly what I was afraid of. I didn't want to be publicly humiliated. My marriage is trending. Gossip sites, tabloids, radio stations, podcasts, and social media can't stop talking about Malik's affair."

"Girl, fuck what anybody gotta say."

"Kierra, you know I hate people in my business. I did some research on Sexy Stackz. Her name is Amber Kelley. She was born in Los Angeles, and she moved to Miami when she was a teenager. She dances for famous rappers, actors, athletes, politicians, and even pastors. She's been rumored to have dated multiple celebrities. According to one of her social media posts, Malik knew she was pregnant. He gave her money for an abortion, and once she refused to go through with it, he blocked her number and blocked her from his social media accounts, and she hasn't been able to get in contact with him. She also claimed that she slept with Malik more than once. She's due to have the baby in August. Malik left all this bullshit out. He's still not being one hundred with me after getting caught."

"That doesn't mean what she says is true. She could be lying. I think you should pause on getting the divorce until you know the facts," Kierra replied.

"What did I do to deserve this? I was faithful and loyal; I cooked, cleaned, and gave him sex and head without him asking for it. I kept my appearance up, took care of my skin and body, dressed nice, and kept my hair done. When he would lose games, feel defeated, and be hard on himself, I was the one who constantly motivated, supported him, and stroked his ego. I did everything a good wife should, and it still wasn't enough. He still cheated. Why her? Is it because her skin is lighter? Is it because she's younger? Does he find her more attractive than me?"

"Ayesha, no. She ain't nothing but a fake-ass Lauren London-looking bitch with a BBL and work done to her titties. You were naturally blessed with ass and titties. You were skinny in high school, but you got more ass than Simone now. You're naturally pretty without makeup, you have a lot going on for yourself, and you're a businesswoman, a wonderful wife, and an amazing mother. She can't compare to you. All men cheat, and some of the most beautiful women in the world still get cheated on, regardless of how good they are.

Malik fucked up, and I'm not justifying his actions, but at the end of the day, you're his wife, and he still loves you, and she ain't nothing but a cum stain trying to extort him. Fuck that bum-ass bitch. I say we go to Miami and have a conversation with her."

"We can't fight a pregnant woman, Kierra. The next thing you know, she'll sue, and we'll end up in jail."

"Who said anything about fighting? I just wanna talk."

"Kierra, there's no *just talking* to you."

Malik stayed elsewhere for about a week and returned home. The girls adored him, and I couldn't deny that he was the dad that every girl wanted to have, and that's why I decided to let him stay at the house. Maliyah and Milan had what I longed for as a child: a father who cared, protected, spoiled, and loved them unconditionally. I didn't want to feel like I was keeping the girls away from him. I also got tired of being asked, *"When is Daddy coming home?"* Although I thought that he wasn't a good husband for what he'd done to me, he was a damn good father. Malik and I slept in separate rooms in our home. We hadn't slept in the same bed since before I found out about his affair. I barely spoke to him; I didn't bother to cook for him, and when he would walk into the same room and try to make small talk, I would leave. Malik tried so hard to make it up to me with gifts. On Valentine's Day, he had our home filled with roses, hired a private chef to cook, and a famous music artist named GeQuan to sing during a candlelight dinner at our house, and Malik gifted me with a diamond Cuban link necklace. I still didn't give him any pussy that night. He bought me a brand-new Mercedes G-Wagon for my birthday, but I was unimpressed. I was still hell-bent on getting that divorce.

2020 was not my year. Not only did my marriage fall apart that year, but COVID-19 tried to destroy my life. The COVID pandemic caused the basketball season to be canceled, my salon to be temporarily shut down, and delays with orders from my website. I felt like I was losing money, but with our savings and Malik's endorsements, we weren't hurting financially. My booming salon was now empty with a *closed* sign on the door. My website was getting negative customer reviews due to delays with their purchases. I lost clientele due to the salon closing. I was afraid that both of my businesses would never recover.

COVID-19 took my family that year. Auntie Angie passed away a week after my birthday. Auntie Angie was diagnosed with Alzheimer's Disease some years before her death. We all had hectic schedules, and when she lived with me, I fired the home care staff that was caring for Auntie Angie because they had let her run out of the house, and it was several hours before West Bloomfield Police found her. We all made the difficult decision to put Auntie Angie in a nursing home. Bloomfield Meadows was a ten-minute drive from my home. I would visit Auntie Angie there almost every day, but visiting was prohibited during the pandemic. Auntie Angie was transferred from Bloomfield Meadows to the nearest hospital, where she passed away from COVID-19. We weren't allowed to visit her at the hospital due to the visitation restrictions, and she passed away alone. We gave her a lovely homegoing service, but the pandemic restricted the number of people attending it. It was just me, Simone, Keith, Elijah, Eric, Malik, and the girls at her service. Imani wasn't in attendance.

One late night in June, I got a phone call.

"May I speak to Ayesha?"

"This is her. Who's speaking?"

"Hey, this is Antoinette, Tony's girlfriend."

"Hey. Is everything okay?"

"No. Tony just passed away in the hospital. He died of COVID. He had been on a ventilator, and between the virus and his asthma, he fought a hard battle."

"Oh my God, I didn't know. I haven't spoken to him in a while."

"I know. You're the first to know of his death. I haven't told Little Tony and Tori yet, and I don't know how to tell them, honestly. Tony didn't have any life insurance, so I'm setting up a GoFundMe account for his funeral expenses."

"Antoinette, you don't have to do that. Whatever the costs are, I'll pay for them. I know things were a bit rocky when he was alive, but that's still my dad. It's the least I can do. Choose whatever funeral home you want. I'll buy him a nice suit to wear, and I'll contact my florist and caterer. We'll have the repass at a nice banquet hall and give him a proper homegoing service."

"Thank you. I want you to know that Tony loved you, and he was so proud of you, Ayesha," Antoinette cried.

When Tony passed away in June of COVID, I cried when he died, but I don't know if I was crying because we would never speak again or if it was because we had issues that we never got the chance to resolve. I wasn't on the best of terms with him before he passed. My father has two other kids. He has twins by Antoinette, a boy and a girl named Tony and Tori. I was envious of them because he was such a great dad to them and very active in their lives, and I didn't get that from him as a child. I saw posts on social media of my father taking Little Tony to his football games and Tori to daddy-daughter dances, and I was very jealous of them. I wasn't close to his other kids, and although he met my daughters, they weren't close to him. Seeing the relationship that he had with Little Tony and Tori angered me. They don't have stories of Tony being a deadbeat, but I do. The last conversation I had with my father was in 2018. I cursed him out for not being the father he should've been. Instead of taking any accountability and apologizing, he blamed Simone for turning me against him, and Simone had nothing to do with how I felt about Tony. Guilt was eating me up when he died because I had so much hatred toward him, and he was gone.

I remember going to my father's funeral, and everyone knew Little Tony and Tori, and I was a stranger to everyone. Sitting in the front pews of the funeral chapel at his service, I was asked to move because the seats were reserved for the immediate family only. The lady didn't know that I was his oldest daughter. I looked at all the pictures in the obituary and saw all the pictures with him, Little Tony, and Tori, and I saw only one picture of him with me, which was taken on the day of my high school graduation. I was Tony's only child for twenty-two years. The twins were born in 2011, and everyone knew that Little Tony and Tori were his kids, but very few people knew that I was his daughter. I was surprised that I was written in his obituary. I was so angry with him for years because of his broken promises, but I've forgiven him and hope he's at peace. Since then, I've established a relationship with his other two children. I've been keeping in contact with them, spending time with them, and being a supportive big sister and positive role model. I know he would want that.

The deaths in my family brought Malik and me closer together. I started to become hesitant about filing for divorce. Auntie Angie adored Malik, and he could do no wrong in her eyes. *"Don't leave him. He's a good man,"* her voice in my head would say.

I started reminiscing about the good times I shared with Malik and how generous he was to my family. Simone started BOB (Babies of Bullets) on the tenth anniversary of my little sister Aaliyah's death. BOB is a non-profit organization that provides support to parents who lost children to gun violence, offering various forms of assistance such as counseling services, support groups, and educational programs to help parents cope with grief and navigate the challenges that arise after the loss of a child to gun violence. Malik donated a lot of money to the organization. Malik also helped Imani with her music career, plugged her with a top music producer in the industry, had connections to local radio stations, put a substantial amount of money towards Imani's marketing and promotion, and helped get Imani's song on the radio in rotation. Aaliyah's death inspired Elijah to get into the criminal justice field and protect the lives of people, especially children. Elijah is a police officer for the city of Detroit. After Elijah got his degree in criminal justice, Malik paid Elijah's student loans, leaving Elijah free from financial educational debt. I reminisced about how he helped my family, the good times we had together, how good he was to our girls, and how he helped me become a businesswoman.

"Malik, this building is perfect for the salon," I said as I walked into a building on West 7 Mile and Livernois Avenue.

"It's alright," Malik smirked as he removed his Buffs from his face.

"You're a hater. This place has D'Goddess written all over it. I told you that I wanted my salon on the Avenue of Fashion. Malik, this is it."

"I got something better than this."

"Boy, bye."

"Baby, hear me out. There's this building on East Jefferson. It's more expensive than this one, but it's close to downtown and Belle Isle. The location will help you attract more regular and high-end clientele. The celebrities from Detroit will come to get serviced. When word gets out that you have big names coming through the salon, everyone in the city will come. The building is bigger than this one, giving you more room for more chairs, which equals more clients. It has a more elegant look to it. You love pink, and with this building that

I'm talking about, I can picture a pink interior, a check-in counter in the front, light-up styling mirrors, wash bowls, leather styling chairs, plush seating, dope-ass manicure tables for the nail station, and the area for facials and waxing will be toward the back. I promise you'll love this place."

"Well, I'll be the judge of that. Let's see it," I replied.

I fell in love with the building on East Jefferson the moment I walked in, and without any hesitation, I decided that it would be the location of D'Goddess Salon and Spa. Malik's vision for the salon's atmosphere became my vision and a reality. I felt like the luckiest woman in the world to have a husband who supported my dreams and made them come true.

As I was reminded of the good times, I decided to give our marriage another chance. We got video counseling from Sylvia and pastoral counseling from Pastor Marcus Whitehill of Prayer and Praise Tabernacle, a megachurch in Detroit. He counseled us before we got married and officiated our wedding ceremony.

"Well, let me first say I'm grateful you both have come here today. It takes courage to confront these challenges head-on, especially when the pain runs deep. Now, I want us to start by acknowledging the hurt and betrayal that's been experienced. Infidelity is a wound that cuts to the core of a marriage, leaving scars that can be incredibly difficult to heal. I also want to affirm the love that brought you together and the commitment you made before each other and before God," Pastor Whitehill said.

"Thanks for meeting with us," I replied.

"Malik, I want to speak to you directly. As a professional athlete, you understand the importance of discipline, dedication, and teamwork. I want to challenge you to apply those same principles to your marriage. Your actions have caused deep pain, but redemption is possible. It will require humility, accountability, and a willingness to put your wife's needs above yours," Pastor Whitehill said.

"I understand. I'll do anything not to lose my wife," Malik replied.

"Ayesha, I want you to know that your feelings are valid. The hurt, the anger, and the confusion are all a natural response to what you've been through. I also see your strength, resilience, and love for your family. Your willingness to fight for your marriage speaks volumes about your character. Now, forgiveness is a journey, and it does not happen overnight, but I believe it's possible with God's grace and with both of your commitment to each other. Counseling, open communication, rebuilding trust, and prayer will be important steps along the way. Remember, marriage is a covenant and a sacred bond between two people and with God. It's worth fighting for, especially when you have two beautiful daughters depending on you both. Let's pray together, seeking guidance and strength for the journey ahead," Pastor Whitehill said.

Malik vowed never to cheat, and I vowed to let go of resentment and anger. We started sleeping in the same bed and making love again. We were in a good space again. Amber had gotten quiet about her pregnancy. She didn't post about it on social media or make any public appearances, which made me think that the whole pregnancy was a lie. I was relieved, and it seemed like the world had forgotten about Malik's affair with Amber.

2020 was one of the worst fucking years of my life. I thought my marriage was ruined; I lost my great-aunt, I lost my dad, and then my mom caught COVID-19, and that scared me to death because I didn't want to lose my mom, but she survived. When my salon reopened, it was a bit chaotic. Some of the stylists who solely depended on the money made at the salon found full-time jobs elsewhere after the salon closed. I had to find new stylists, and I had to come up with different marketing techniques, such as implementing discounts and specials to gain new clientele. I had a promotional deal on the website where everything was half off, not to mention the virus was still spreading. To prevent more stylists and customers from getting sick and avoid more appointment cancellations, we took extreme measures to ensure that everything in the salon was sanitized, made customers and stylists wear face masks, and even did temperature checks. That year's highlight and good memory was finally getting together with my family for a New Year's Eve party at our home. It seemed like the only time we saw each other that year was at funerals. After quarantining, it had been months since my family and Malik's family had gotten together for something good.

CHAPTER 18

Let It Go

It was the beginning of 2021, and I decided not to dwell on what went wrong the prior year. I was leaving 2020 in 2020. I wanted this year to be an excellent year for me, and a year of rebuilding my businesses, marriage, and life. Three weeks into the new year, shit hit the fan.

After disappearing from the face of the earth, Miss Amber Sexy Stackz is back. Here we go again. This time, Amber has an almost six-month-old baby girl. Khloe Dior Kelley was born on August 8, 2020. Amber posted a live video with Khloe, demanding that Malik take a DNA test to prove that he's Khloe's father. Amber continued to bash Malik on social media live, calling him a deadbeat father, claiming that he had never visited Khloe, and threatening to sue him for child support. That video went viral. From there, Amber began doing television, podcast, and radio interviews and planned to join the cast of the hit reality show *Basketball Baby Mamas of Miami*. It gets worse. People continuously discussed the similarities when comparing baby pictures of my daughters and Khloe. It didn't help that Khloe had a striking resemblance to Milan. People were now speculating that Malik was indeed the father of Khloe. My marriage became gossip news again, and it was time for me to have a woman-to-woman conversation with Amber.

Malik continued to deny that he was Khloe's father. I told Malik I needed space, but didn't tell him where I was going. I flew to Miami and contacted a friend who owned a bar there. I needed to meet Amber somewhere private. The bar didn't open until late evening, making it the perfect place to meet up with Amber while avoiding cameras and paparazzi. Amber and I met at the bar before noon. I was staring at the woman who fucked my husband and claimed to have his child.

"I'm not trying to break up a happy home," Amber said.

"How can you be sure that your daughter belongs to my husband?"

"I'm sure that Malik Davis is my daughter's father. Let's be honest. If you knew there wasn't a chance in hell that he was the father, you wouldn't have contacted me and flown down here."

"When and where did you meet my husband?"

"I met him in May of two thousand nineteen at a playoff game here in Miami. I had courtside seats. It was game three, and Detroit lost. I was rooting for my city to win and happy about our victory, but I told him that I was a fan of his. He invited me to his hotel room and told me he needed to relieve some stress. I'm quite sure you know what happened next."

"That's funny. Malik said that he met you at Cedric Sterling's bachelor party, and that was in late two thousand nineteen," I replied.

"Cedric's bachelor party was not our first encounter. I met Malik months before the party. After our first night together, I gave Malik my business card. He would hit me up every time he came to town. Malik hired me to dance at Cedric's party and paid me quite well, plus tips, for the private performance I gave Malik later that night."

"There's no secret that Malik Davis is a married man. You knew he was married. You knew about me and our family. How could you?"

"He knew he was married. How could he?"

"It's sad because you're a gorgeous girl, and you did not need to stoop so low to sleep with someone else's husband."

"I know things your husband likes that you don't, and I do things you won't. Malik enjoys more than one girl at a time in the bedroom. I remember when we had a threesome at his place in Miami. I wish you had joined us. I would've had fun tasting you. If you don't believe that I've been to his place, well, Malik has a blue pool table. The living room has gray-colored furniture, not too far from the balcony. It was the same balcony where he had me bent over as I enjoyed the beautiful view of the blue water. The master bedroom is located on the far left. I never went in there because Malik kept it locked. He had enough respect for you not to fuck me in your bed."

"You're nothing but a high-profile ho. You must be proud to sell pussy for a living."

"I am proud because I'm making money, and it's the same pussy that your baller-ass husband paid for."

"You're fucking pathetic."

"I'm pathetic? I'm not the one losing sleep at night. You lose sleep every night, wondering if Malik is fucking other bitches. Meanwhile, I get to count my money and sleep peacefully. I would hate to be in your shoes. I feel sorry for you."

"You feel sorry for me? Bitch, I feel sorry for you. You're the one who has to open your legs to get ahead. I don't know how they do things here in Miami, but I'm from Detroit. You've heard the stories about my city. Detroit is really about that life, and if I didn't have so much to lose and the sense that God gave me, I would fuck you up."

"Is that a threat?"

"I don't make threats; I make promises, but you're not even worth the risk."

"I'm worth every risk. In case you didn't know, I'm the baddest bitch in Miami. I can have any nigga I want, including a nigga with a bigger bag than yours. I don't want Malik. I want him to take care of our daughter. It's unfair that he's a father to his other daughters and not to Khloe. Malik knows that he's Khloe's father, and that's why he gave me abortion money and hush money to keep quiet. Malik is toxic, and you can keep pretending like you're happy, but you're not. You're miserable as fuck. You pretend that you and Malik are a power couple, but deep down, you feel powerless. You can't stand to see my face. Seeing my daughter makes you sick because when you see her, you know the truth. Please take my advice. Chase the bag like me and stop chasing him. He doesn't deserve you. I don't know if he made you sign a prenup, but go for half of everything, start over, and live your best life. You deserve better. Tell Malik I'll see his ass in court," Amber said before leaving the bar.

I left Miami feeling furious. My anger was intense, my heart was pounding, and it felt like my head was about to explode. I couldn't get home fast enough to chew Malik's ass out.

"Oh, so you can't answer the fucking phone? I've been calling you! Where were you?" Malik yelled when I arrived home.

"I was in Miami."

"For what?"

"I met with Amber. She told me everything. You're a fucking liar.'

"You went behind my back?"

"Malik, don't you dare do that! You went behind my back when you cheated! You didn't meet her at Cedric's bachelor party. You met her during the playoffs in Miami, months before Cedric's party! No wonder you got eliminated in the playoffs. The Detroit Spark Plugs played seven games against the Miami Waves in the playoffs that season, and maybe if your head was in the game and not between Amber's fucking legs, you wouldn't have lost! You brought that bitch into our condo, but you didn't fuck her in our bed. At least you gave me *some* respect," I said in a sarcastic tone.

"That bitch is a fucking liar! She never came to the condo! I can't believe this shit."

"What can't you believe, Malik? You can't believe that your lies have caught up with you? Stop fucking lying to me! She described the condo, from the blue pool table to the color of our furniture! She even knew where our bedroom was! For God's sake, our children sleep there, and you brought some whores there! Yeah, I heard you love threesomes. I wouldn't ever allow you to bring another woman into our bed, and you know it."

"What do you want me to do?"

"You can start by taking a DNA test. If you're the father of that bitch's baby, you can move her and your child into the condo. I will never step foot in that place again!"

Malik agreed to take a DNA test, and it was determined that Malik was Khloe's father. I was devastated. I went through a whirlwind of emotions. The situation was a complete mess. Malik gave Amber a substantial amount of money monthly, more than enough for Khloe's expenses. However, Amber demanded more, and he always argued with her. Amber captured screenshots of their arguments and sent them to gossip blogs, and Malik was back in the headlines. Among the leaked messages was one from Malik to Amber: ***"I wish you had the fucking abortion."*** That didn't help his reputation. His reputation took another blow when Amber accused Malik of domestic violence following their altercation in Miami. Malik swore that Amber's accusations of him physically assaulting her were false. Although he was never arrested, he still had to pay Amber a nice fee to drop the charges. I was sick of Malik's baby mama drama bullshit.

When Basketball Baby Mamas of Miami aired, Amber's storyline was about her affair with Malik, raising Khloe, and working on her rap career. Strangers would approach me at the grocery store, talking about the latest episode and how they felt sorry for me in front of my children. I didn't allow my daughters to watch shows like that or any shows that weren't age-appropriate. I couldn't take my children to school without other parents staring at me. I almost got into a fight with another parent at the school because they asked me if Malik was still sleeping with Sexy Stackz, and my youngest daughter was standing beside me. I almost lost my temper, could've gone to jail, and could've gotten my daughters expelled that day for my actions. My daughters attended a private school in Bloomfield Hills, and I was considering homeschooling, something I'd never considered before. I would hear clients whispering and laughing at me at the salon. I closed my personal social media accounts and kept my phone on DND. It wasn't personal, but I needed to distance myself from family and even Kierra, so I shut down from the world.

As much as I hate to admit it, Amber was right. I was so unhappy in my marriage. Amber and Khloe were constant reminders of the pain Malik caused. Sylvia was right. Money isn't everything. The money and success could not heal my broken heart. It couldn't fix the pain. I didn't care about his money. I was a successful businesswoman who saved money throughout the years and would be okay financially without him. I might've been able to forgive Malik for cheating, but having a baby with another woman? That's where I draw the line. See, there's a difference between just cheating and making a baby. If Malik had hooked up with Amber and she didn't get pregnant, and he was completely honest with me, we could've possibly moved on and never looked back. But now there's a child involved, another family in the mix, and my daughters have a little sister out there. That's not something you can brush under the rug. I was ready to let it go.

"Malik, I'm filing for divorce, and I'm going through with it this time."

"Ayesha, not this shit again. What the fuck do you want now? Diamonds? A new whip? A new crib? How about I take you on a trip? Anywhere you wanna go. How can I fix this shit?"

"That's the problem, Malik. You think that money can fix everything, but it can't. Every time you fuck up, you throw your money around. I'm calling my lawyer first thing in the morning. I want this done and over with."

"Are you fucking serious right now?"

"I'm serious as fuck."

"I can't take back what I did, Ayesha! Khloe is my daughter, just like Maliyah and Milan. I fucked up, I'm sorry. What more do you want me to do?"

"There's nothing more you can do, Malik. How dare you get mad at me for wanting to end this over your infidelity and lies? I shouldn't have to compete with another woman for my husband! I can't go anywhere in public without being questioned about your side chick and love child!"

"I come home to you. I take good care of my daughters, and I take good care of you, and you shouldn't have any complaints."

"I have several complaints. You're a great father and provider, but you're lacking as a husband. If the shoe were on the other foot, could I have fucked who I wanted, gotten pregnant by another man, and caused the same hurt and humiliation that you've caused me? Imagine if I fucked the rappers, *basketball players*, and actors who were all in my DM. You have daughters, Malik. You wouldn't want men doing what you did to me to them. I'm not Juanita. You will not do what Maurice did to that woman for years. I'm not a doormat like she is."

"Don't talk about my parents."

"The apple doesn't fall far from the tree. You're just like Maurice."

"Seriously? I do everything for you, and nothing I do is ever good enough for your ass. After all the shit I've done for you and your damn family, and this is the appreciation I get? You wouldn't be living this lifestyle if it wasn't for me; you wouldn't have that salon or shit. It's bitches out here who would be lucky to have me, so you should be counting your mothafucking blessings. Without me, you would still be living on Euclid, driving that raggedy-ass whip, and doing hair at that raggedy-ass shop on Six Mile, working for somebody else. I'm the reason why you came up in the first place. You need me."

"Nigga, I don't need you or your money. Thank you for helping me, but I would've made it without you."

"You'll never find another nigga like me. I promise you that."

"You've always been an arrogant mothafucka. Fuck you," I replied.

Malik had never put his hands on me, but I thought he would that night. He knew I meant business this time and that our marriage was officially over. Malik had all the classic signs of a narcissist—never taking responsibility for his actions, no empathy for others, always acting like he was the center of the universe, constantly needing praise, and thinking he deserved everything handed to him on a silver platter. I don't hate and will always love him, but I'm not one to stand by someone who feels like they can do whatever they please because of their wealth, fame, and status. I would've rather lived a middle-class lifestyle with a faithful husband than be rich and married to a cheater.

Malik had his father's characteristics. Like his father, Malik lacked self-control. His father, Maurice, was an older caramel version of Malik. He was tall, well-dressed, handsome, and a ladies' man. Maurice aspired to be a basketball player but ended up working in the automotive industry after high school. A few years later, Maurice married a beautiful woman named Juanita, who had beautiful chocolate-colored skin, long hair, and dimples. They had two children together, Camille and Malik. Like Malik, Maurice was a great provider and father, but he was also a cheater and a liar. Malik spoke so highly of his dad. He idolized Maurice, always wanted to be just like him, and did everything to impress him. Maurice taught Malik that cheating is what men do, and as long as you're a good provider, you're a good husband. Juanita knew that Maurice had been cheating for years, but she stayed by his side. Malik thought that I would never leave him, like Juanita never left Maurice. Malik underestimated me.

When we first got married, I made it clear to Malik: whatever he did, don't let me find out about it, don't bring me home any diseases, and don't bring me home any babies. He never brought me home any diseases, but I had to find out about another woman, and he failed me on the baby part. Through it all, we shared beautiful moments and made two beautiful daughters. I have beautiful memories that I will forever cherish, but our fairytale ended.

After my divorce was finalized, I immediately had a tattoo cover-up done, replacing Malik's name with a rose design. My divorce didn't get finalized until December 2022, a year and a half later, because the COVID pandemic caused backlogs in the court system, and Malik didn't want to sign the fucking papers and was being a petty-ass nigga. It was like he was trying to punish me and hold me hostage in that marriage. I didn't wait for him to sign any fucking papers before I moved out of our house. I purchased a home for under five hundred thousand in a subdivision in West Bloomfield, less than fifteen minutes away. I downsized to a colonial-style house, and my spoiled-ass daughters hated it. I remember Maliyah saying, *"Mom, I don't wanna live in this house."* My new home wasn't half the square feet or as luxurious, and it didn't have a saltwater pool, spiral staircase, porcelain floors, marble bathroom, or lakefront view like the home I shared with Malik, but none of that mattered. The house I purchased was nice and cozy, with a patio and a big backyard in a peaceful neighborhood. Most of all, the house was mine, and I had peace. Malik was mad as fuck when I moved out. I moved out while he was out of town, and when he came back, the girls and I were gone. He cursed me out badly and even accused me of kidnapping his daughters. Can you believe that shit?

The most challenging part about splitting from Malik was how it affected the girls. Maliyah and Milan adore their dad; they're both daddy's girls and crazy about Malik. It was tough explaining to them that Mommy and Daddy weren't together anymore and that we were getting a divorce. They took our separation pretty hard, and I had to put them in counseling. Co-parenting with Malik can be challenging at times. Malik is a great dad, but he's more of a fun parent. He gives the girls whatever they want, doesn't raise his voice, and there aren't many rules when they're with him. If the girls want pizza and ice cream for breakfast, Malik will give them pizza and ice cream. When they're with him, there's no bedtime schedule; they play on their iPads as long as they want, don't have to eat their vegetables, and he allows them to binge on junk food. I make them eat their vegetables, I have restrictions on how long they're allowed to be on their iPads, they have a bedtime schedule, I don't let them eat a bunch of junk, and when they act out, I'm not hesitant to discipline them. At the beginning of the separation, the girls would cry when they had to leave after visiting Malik and come home with me. Malik used that against me, saying that I was messing them up by divorcing him and claiming they wanted to live with him full-time, and told me that he was going for full custody. Malik just said that to get under my skin. He didn't attempt to go for full custody because he knew damn well that his schedule was too hectic. Who was going to raise the girls while he was on the road, other than me? A nanny? His parents? Nigga, please. The judge granted us joint legal custody, with me receiving sole physical custody of the girls.

The divorce wasn't as messy as people might've thought. Malik and I didn't fight or bicker over assets, possessions, money, or anything else. I wasn't the vindictive, scorned, bitter woman who tried to go after all his money. What was his is his, what was mine is mine, and we mutually agreed on everything. My divorce may not have been messy, but it was still hard. I never wanted my marriage to end the way it did. I went through a period of depression. My divorce became headline news, discussed on talk shows, radio, podcasts, gossip blogs, and across social media. Negative content is what sells in the entertainment world. People love mess and hot gossip. When Malik and I were happily married and had a happy family, making public appearances, riding on floats at the Thanksgiving Parade in Detroit with our children, and smiling, I didn't get nearly as many offers to do interviews. I was even offered book deals after my divorce, but I was never offered a book deal before that. I became more known for being the ex-wife of a cheating basketball star who impregnated a known jump-off than a successful Black entrepreneur, and that infuriated me.

Every year, D'Goddess Salon and Spa hosts a back-to-school event, providing free hairstyling services, free bookbags, and school supplies to underprivileged children aged five to seventeen. Over the years, Malik and I have donated money to schools in Detroit and organized many charitable events for the city, but no one talks about any of that. People are more concerned about what happened in our marriage. Malik has made history as one of the greatest Detroit Spark Plugs players of all time and has broken records, but the entertainment world continuously talks about his extramarital affair. It's like the world is obsessed with the bad and doesn't give a fuck about the good. I have no problems doing interviews, but what I won't do is sit on someone's platform for an hour, talking about my failed marriage and badmouthing my ex-husband to entertain the world. Instead, I'll gladly discuss my journey as a businesswoman, promote my salon, website, and hair care line, and discuss any plans for the future.

The Detroit Spark Plugs won the basketball championship in June 2023. Ironically, the celebration was at the Luxury Hills Banquet Center, where Malik and I had gotten married. I stared at the venue's dance floor, trying to hold back tears, reminiscing about our first dance at our wedding reception. We danced to the song *Spend My Life With You* by Eric Benét and Tamia.

Malik approached me and said, "I'm surprised to see you here."

"Malik, we agreed to remain friends for the girls' sake, and as a *friend*, I had to support and congratulate you. You played your ass off this season, and you deserved that MVP title."

"Thanks. You got any plans later on?"

"Yes. My plans include going to bed and getting some sleep," I replied.

"I was thinking about coming through to see you."

"Malik, I don't think that's a good idea. I wish you the best. You take care of yourself," I said as I kissed him on the cheek and walked away.

"You looking good, shawty," Cedric said to me in his Southern accent.

"Thanks, Cedric."

Cedric Sterling was one of Malik's teammates. He was from the Dirty South and not the Dirty D. Cedric was tall, a shade lighter than me, with tattoos and a thick, neatly trimmed beard. Cedric was fine as fuck, but he was also married with two kids.

"You a good one for showing up for Leek."

"Malik and I are cordial. Regardless of the circumstances, I'm proud of his victory. Let me ask you a question, Cedric. I know it doesn't matter anymore, but to my understanding, Sexy Stackz was at your party. Did you know what was going on between her and Malik?"

"Yeah. I wanted to hit Stackz first, but Leek beat me to the finish line. She was bad as fuck, but she ain't got shit on you, shawty. Leek fucked up big time," Cedric said as he stared me up and down, rubbing his hands together, licking his lips, and admiring my body.

"How are your wife and kids? Jessica is your wife's name, right?"

"My family doing good. Jess and the kids couldn't make it. She had a death in the family. I can't judge Leek. We all got sins. Shit, I do my thang. Don't get me wrong; I love my wife, but I fasho love pussy."

"It's getting late. I need to head home. It was nice talking to you, Ced."

Cedric gave me his phone number and said, "Lock me in. No disrespect to Leek, but you a single woman now. I wanna know what you taste like."

"You're married, Cedric. Bye," I said before I left.

I was single, divorced, in the healing process, and preparing for another chapter in my life. I was also horny as fuck. I hadn't had sex in a while, but I couldn't take Cedric's offer. I refused to fuck Malik's homeboy. I was at home when I received a text from Malik.

"Open the door," the text said.

I took another sip of my wine, set the glass on the kitchen counter, fixed my robe, and headed toward the front door. Malik didn't tell me that he was coming over. He had some fucking nerve, popping up at my house at three in the morning.

"Malik, what do you want?"

"Oh, I can't come in?"

"No."

"We need to talk. It's important."

"You're drunk. Go home, Malik."

"I'll make it quick."

"Come in, but make it quick."

"Are the girls here?"

"They're upstairs asleep. Why are you here? You said you'd make it quick."

"What's the rush? Oh, I get it. That nigga Cedric must be sliding through, or maybe he already left."

"What?"

"Don't play fucking dumb with me, Ayesha. I saw you talking to that nigga at the party. Cedric is a snake, and that nigga will fuck anybody's bitch. Tell the truth, did you fuck him?"

"First of all, Malik, I'm not your bitch, and I don't owe you any fucking explanation. We're divorced. You don't get to pop up at my house that I paid for and question me."

"I can't believe you fucked one of my niggas. That's some real ho-ass shit. You out here acting thirsty as fuck."

"I didn't fuck Cedric! As a matter of fact, why am I explaining myself to you? Get the fuck out, Malik! Now!"

"I'm sorry. I miss you," Malik said as he started kissing my neck.

"Malik, stop," I moaned.

As Malik kissed and sucked on my neck, his hands roamed over my body. He caressed my breasts until my nipples hardened, palmed and rubbed my ass, then slid his fingers between my legs, gently massaging my clit. I could feel myself getting wet. I still yearned for Malik sexually, and he knew exactly how to ignite my fire.

"You ain't done with me," Malik said as he grabbed my face and stuck his tongue in my mouth.

We kissed passionately as if the time apart had made us yearn for each other more than ever. Every touch and caress felt electrifying, igniting a fiery connection that revealed how deeply we craved each other. Malik then picked me up and sat me on the steps. He spread my legs and licked and sucked on my clit as I gripped the stairwell, one leg draped over his shoulder, eating me like I was the most delicious piece of fruit he'd ever tasted, while I ran my fingers through every wave of his taper haircut. But before I reached orgasm, Malik said, "You know this will always be my pussy."

Malik picked me up, carried me to the bedroom, and gently laid me on my back. He then positioned my legs over his shoulders, and with passion, he entered me. I clawed at his back as the intensity of our lovemaking brought tears to my eyes. My tears were a mix of overwhelming pleasure from Malik being inside me, the pain he had caused, and the deep love I still felt for him. We made love until we both reached climax.

A few days later, I decided to fly Simone and the girls, along with myself, to California for a getaway. California was one of my happy places. We spent time at the Santa Monica Pier, soaking in the beautiful weather, atmosphere, and vibes.

"They remind me so much of how you and Imani used to play together," Simone said about Maliyah and Milan.

"Except Milan is more like me, and Maliyah is more like Imani," I replied.

"I need to ask you something. Tell me the truth. Did you sleep with Malik the other night?"

"Ma, why would you ask me that?"

"Because Cream and Cocoa saw Malik in the bed with you."

Simone playfully nicknamed Maliyah *Cream* and Milan *Cocoa* because Maliyah's lighter complexion resembled French vanilla pastry cream, while Milan's skin tone was the rich color of natural cocoa powder.

"Don't lie to me. You did sleep with him, didn't you?"

"Okay, I slept with Malik."

"Ayesha, what are you doing? Do you even know?"

"What's the big deal?"

"The big deal is that you should be focusing on maintaining a co-parenting relationship with Malik and not engaging in a sexual one. It's toxic, and you're confusing the girls. The girls think you and Malik are back together. How are you supposed to move forward when stuck in the past? How are you supposed to heal when you can't let go of the person who hurt you and caused you pain? Stop acting so dickmatized."

"Ma, I am not dickmatized."

"That's not what Malik thinks. If he can show up to the house you paid for whenever he wants and have sex with you whenever he feels like it, then you're giving him too much power over you. It's time to set boundaries."

"You're right. I can't move forward if I keep moving backward. It's unbelievable how life can change. I'm divorced, and Kierra is married now."

"I'm glad that she finally married Rashad. He's a good guy," Simone said. "Ayesha, I need to talk to you about something," Simone continued.

"What is it?"

"I went to the doctor, and I have cancer. I eat right, I exercise, I haven't smoked in over fifteen years, I rarely drink anymore, and if I do, it's a glass of wine or champagne on special occasions. I'm making all the healthy decisions in life, and I wasn't expecting any diagnosis like this."

"What? Have you told Keith? What about Imani or Elijah?"

"I haven't told anyone. You're the only one who knows, and I don't need you telling anyone. I'll be the one to share the news. If I'm being honest, I'm not afraid of anything. God has the final say. I refuse to let this disease make me or break me. Whenever God calls me home, I hope my baby enters my arms. It's been almost twenty years, and I miss Aaliyah more and more every day," Simone said.

"Ma, please don't talk like this. I know of some incredible doctors who will help you beat this. Fuck cancer," I cried.

It's always something. If it isn't one thing, it's another. The thought of losing my mother was unimaginable to me. She played a vital role in shaping me into the entrepreneur I am today. I prepared to help her take every measure in her fight against cancer. Cancer was a battle that she was not going to lose.

Growing up in the hood and being raised by a single mother instilled in me a determination to overcome adversity. The experiences of the hood, coupled with personal tragedies, fueled my drive to break free from the limitations of my circumstances. The financial setbacks brought on by the pandemic served as a turning point for me. During this challenging period, I decided to leverage my passion and expertise to establish Queen's Crown Hair Care in 2022. Queen's Crown is my hair care product line, which offers products such as hair growth oil, shampoo, conditioner, and edge control, and it became a testament to my resilience and ability to turn adversity into opportunity. Being a go-getter has always been my approach to life. I firmly believe in preparing for the unexpected in today's dynamic world. With this mindset, I've diversified my sources of income, ensuring that I have multiple revenue streams. I've strategically built a multifaceted business model from the salon to an online platform and now with hair care products. The struggles of my upbringing motivated me to become an entrepreneur. It taught me the importance of self-reliance and creating one's path to success. Through hard work, determination, and a commitment to overcoming challenges, I have transformed my life and built a thriving business empire.

Later that summer, two close friends of a non-profit organization dedicated to hosting various community events, including back-to-school initiatives and toy drives, orchestrated the grandest pop-up shop event in the city, titled *Entrepreneurs of Colour*, held at Huntington Place, formerly known as Cobo Hall. I got to know these amazing women back in high school when I was dating Chase. They attended Cass Tech alongside Chase, and although my relationship with him didn't last, my friendship with these ladies did. They extended the honor of being a guest speaker at the event to me, which I eagerly accepted. I didn't stop there. I made sure to lend my support to numerous vendors. After all, we all thrive on support. Among the vendors was a childhood friend showcasing her book.

"It's good to see you. Congratulations on your new book. You know I came to purchase a copy, and I want it signed. You're a writer and music producer. What can't you do?"

"I can't do hair like you," she replied.

"And I can't make beats like you. I just purchased some artwork from your sister. I see that she's a vendor here as well. Where's your best friend? I would love for her to design a dress for me," I said.

"She couldn't make it. She's on her honeymoon in Greece, living her best life, but thank you for supporting me. It means a lot, Ayesha."

"Don't mention it. You always have my support. Give your best friend my business card and tell her to contact me."

As I stood among hundreds of entrepreneurs, dreamers, and ambitious people of color, preparing to give my speech, I wanted this speech to be special.

"Ladies and gentlemen, esteemed guests, fellow entrepreneurs, and aspiring dreamers, I stand before you today as a testament to the power of resilience, determination, and the unwavering belief that we can shape our destinies. Like many of you, my journey has been filled with challenges and setbacks, but I am here to share a story of triumph, growth, and pursuing dreams against all odds. My name is Ayesha Davis, and I am the proud owner of D'Goddess Salon and Spa, D'Goddess Hair Collection, and Queen's Crown Hair Care products. My journey didn't begin with success; it started in the heart of struggle. I was raised by a single mother, a woman of immense strength who instilled in me the values of hard work, perseverance, and the importance of never giving up. In the face of adversity, she showed me that it's not about where you start but where you choose to go. Tragedy struck my life when I lost my precious six-year-old sister to a senseless act of violence. The pain was deep, and the road ahead seemed impossible. Yet, in those darkest moments, I found the strength to turn my grief into a driving force, a motivation to build something lasting, something that would honor her memory. I went through a divorce, a chapter in my life that tested my resilience once again, but instead of letting it define me, I used it as an opportunity for self-discovery and growth. I emerged more vigorous, with a clearer vision of my goal."

"Today, I am not just an entrepreneur but a symbol of possibility. Please look at me and see that your circumstances do not determine your future. The hood I grew up in, the losses I faced, and the hardships I endured were not roadblocks but stepping stones to my success. The journey to entrepreneurship is not a smooth path. It's filled with twists, turns, and unexpected detours. But it is in those challenges that we discover our true strength and resilience. Each setback is an opportunity to rise, learn, and return even more vital."

"To the dreamers in this room, I want you to understand that your past does not define your dreams; they are shaped by your actions today. It doesn't matter where you start; what matters is the direction in which you are headed. Your dreams are valid, and your potential is limitless. As we gather here at the Entrepreneurs of Colour event, let us celebrate diversity, determination, and the belief that any specific background does not confine entrepreneurship. Embrace your uniqueness, let it fuel your creativity, and remember that your story is an essential part of the rich tapestry of entrepreneurship. In the face of adversity, let us not forget the power within us to transform challenges into opportunities."

"As you pursue your dreams, surround yourself with a community that uplifts and supports you, just as we do today. So, my fellow dreamers, stand tall, embrace your journey, and know each step forward is a victory. You can shape your destiny, and your dreams are worth pursuing. Detroit, let's show the world that from the ashes of adversity, we can rise and build something truly extraordinary. Thank you, and may your entrepreneurial journey be filled with triumphs, growth, and unyielding determination."

After I finished my speech, the audience responded with a huge round of applause.

CHAPTER 19

Imani's Story

Currently, business is thriving, Maliyah and Milan are keeping me busy and blossoming into stunning young women, and Malik and I sustain an amicable co-parenting dynamic. This fall, I'm releasing my first book, a memoir of my life, titled *The Book of Ayesha*. Simone is bravely battling cancer with her husband and children by her side. Kierra is anticipating the arrival of a baby boy with her husband, Rashad. I can't wait to meet my godson. Elijah remains dedicated to his noble duty as a police officer, protecting the community and residents of Detroit, and Imani is making moves in her music career.

Speaking of Imani, she was a featured guest on the popular internet podcast *No Filter, No Limits*. Tiffani Blake, renowned as the celebrity gossip queen, hosted No Filter, No Limits. I was not the biggest fan of Tiffani because she had a lot to say about me on her show when I went through my shit with Malik. The sole reason I reached for my laptop to watch her show was to see Imani. As usual, Imani looked stunning. Her makeup was glamorous, her clothes were fabulous, and not a strand of her hair was out of place.

[Tiffani Blake:] This is No Filter, No Limits, where we have no filter, and nothing is off limits. I'm your host, Tiffani Blake, and today, I'm interviewing a very special guest. This young lady is an award-winning singer, songwriter, and fashionista. You've heard her songs, seen her on television, and seen her rock shows. Please give it up for Detroit's own, Imani! Welcome.

[Imani:] Thanks for having me.

[Tiffani Blake:] To those who are watching, make sure you like and subscribe to the channel. Imani, you've topped the charts, you've done tours, you've done features with chart-topping artists, and you are showing the world that Detroit has true talent. How old were you when you discovered your musical talent?

[Imani:] I was five. It was nineteen ninety-six, and my mama used to play the song *Grapevyne* by Brownstone. She'd always have that song on repeat because it was her absolute favorite. She played it so often that I ended up knowing every single word. My mama used to do hair at home, and one day, while she was playing that song, styling someone's hair, I started singing it. My mama and her client were blown away, even though I was too young to be singing that.

[Tiffani Blake:] Wow. That's amazing. Shoutout to Nicci Gilbert, the lead singer of the group, who is also from Detroit. Who did you inherit your singing skills from? Did your mom sing?

[Imani:] No. My mama did hair, and my sister inherited that talent. I inherited my singing talent from my daddy's side of the family. My daddy's mother and sister were both blessed with vocal skills. I can sing, but I don't have anything on my grandma and auntie.

[Tiffani Blake:] That's dope. Did your dad sing?

[**Imani:**] No. My daddy was a big-time dope dealer and a respected figure in the streets. He passed away when I was only two.

[**Tiffani Blake:**] I'm sorry to hear that. Tell me a bit about how you got started in the music business.

[**Imani:**] As a kid, I sang in the choir at church and in the choir in school. My auntie started managing me when I was a teenager. She had me performing at shows, recording, and singing hooks for rap artists around the city. I performed at talent shows, open mics, bars, clubs, Northland Mall, Eastland Mall, skating rinks, and Hart Plaza, and I performed in other states, all before the age of nineteen. When my auntie passed away in 2010, my career started sinking. She was the one who invested time and money in me, got me booked for shows, covered travel expenses, and paid for studio time. I was making minimum wage and couldn't afford studio time. I thought my career was over when my auntie died. She believed in me, taught me stage presence, and schooled me on the music game. I had a closer relationship with her than anyone else in my family. Once I started to get my career back on track, that's when I started dropping mixtapes. I was one of the few singers in the city who dropped mixtapes at that time, and eventually, I got signed.

[**Tiffani Blake:**] You admitted in another interview that you danced at a strip club when you were younger. How did you become a stripper?

[**Imani:**] I was working at a clothing store, making minimum wage, and couldn't afford studio time because I had to pay bills and buy groceries. My friend told me how much she made dancing at the strip club and told me to audition. I auditioned for the owner, and the owner was impressed, so I started working that night.

[**Tiffani Blake:**] What strip club did you work at?

[Imani:] I worked at Queen of Spades on Michigan Avenue. I became the highest-paid dancer at the club. I made more money in one night from dancing than I did in two weeks working in retail. I had money to pay for studio time and record an album, buy a new wardrobe for shows, shoot videos, and get my career back on track. If a celebrity came to a strip club in Detroit, they came to Queen of Spades. Queen of Spades was known for having the prettiest dancers and the best food. I made good money from dancing, but when the celebrities came to the club, I wanted to sing on stage and showcase my real talent, and that's what I did.

[Tiffani Blake:] Did working at the club help you get your name out there?

[Imani:] Yeah, because I was able to meet and network with people, but I never intended on being a stripper for long. It was a quick and good hustle, but I wasn't planning on retiring from stripping. I danced for money, but I never sold any pussy for money. Don't get it twisted, y'all.

[Tiffani Blake:] When it comes to music, who are your influences?

[Imani:] I love Aaliyah. I love her style and voice, and I wanted to dance like her and everything. My mama named my youngest sister after Aaliyah. My mama used to play a lot of Anita Baker, and that's how I became a fan. I performed one of Anita Baker's songs at my sister's wedding. My grandma put me up on Aretha Franklin, Stevie Wonder, The Clark Sisters, and The Winans. I've always been told that I have an old soul.

[Tiffani Blake:] Those are all Detroit legends. What was one of the biggest moments of your career?

[Imani:] One of the biggest moments of my career was rocking the stage at the Fox Theatre. I always told my auntie that I would perform at the Fox. I've performed at the LCA, and that was a big moment for me, but before the LCA was built, my dream was to perform at the Fox. It was too bad that my auntie didn't live to see it.

[Tiffani Blake:] Some might find it challenging to work with you.

[Imani:] My auntie told me a long time ago that this is a dirty business and that people will try to take advantage of me, especially because I'm a woman. Desiree didn't lie when she said that. If I'm allowing people to take advantage of me and walk all over me, I'm easy to work with. But because I refuse to be a doormat, they call me a diva, a bitch, and they say I'm difficult to work with. I'm the easiest person to work with because all I ask for is one thing.

[Tiffani Blake:] What's that?

[Imani:] All I ask for is respect. Respect my time, respect my talent, and respect me as an artist. If I give you a price, either you pay it or keep it moving. Don't try to fuck me over at the end of the night. Here's a prime example. I did a show on New Year's Eve in Detroit. If you know, you know. The promoter was fine with my price, and we had an agreement. I performed, but my money came up short at the end of the night. The cover charge at the club was four times the regular cover charge that night, and there was money made from the door. Why is my money coming up short when the crowd was at capacity? That crowd came to see me. The bar made a lot of money, the DJ was from the radio station, and he got paid, and the host was a popular comedian, and he got paid, but where's my money? The next day, the promoter issued a statement, saying that I was rude and unprofessional and gave a sloppy performance. There's footage of that show. There was nothing sloppy about my performance. How was I unprofessional? I didn't show up to the club late or start my performance late, and if I was rude, it was because I was being short-changed. When you stand up for yourself and speak up, they don't like that in this business, and they will try to smear you. Cash is the only form of payment that I accept. I don't accept checks, credit cards, or coke.

[**Tiffani Blake:**] Coke?

[**Imani:**] Yes, coke, and not the kind you drink. There are a lot of cokeheads in this business, and they're fine with accepting powder as payment, but I don't snort that shit. Fuck that, pay me.

[**Tiffani Blake:**] Are you saying that some people in the industry accept cocaine as payment?

[**Imani:**] That's exactly what I'm saying. Cocaine is a hell of a drug. You can't do that to me. As Kash Doll would say, *run me my money.*

[**Tiffani Blake:**] I love Kash Doll; shoutout to her. She's gorgeous, just like you. I must ask. Have you had any work done? Have you had any BBLs? Any boob jobs? Any work done to your face?

[**Imani:**] I've never had any work done on my face or body, and I have nothing against people who do.

[**Tiffani Blake:**] So your ass is real?

[**Imani:**] Yes, my ass is real. As you see, my ass and thigh ratio add up. My mama and my sister got ass for decades. It runs in the family.

[**Tiffani Blake:**] Why were you dropped from your record label?

[**Imani:**] You tell me.

[Tiffani Blake:] It's quite surprising that you got dropped from the label, especially considering the success of your debut album, *The Book of Imani*. Did they call you in for a meeting? How were you notified?

[Imani:] I received a phone call.

[Tiffani Blake:] Were you surprised?

[Imani:] I was at first because I was one of the most popular artists on the label, and my first album did so well, but what I've learned in this business is that no one is irreplaceable. When they dropped me from the label, Paris Janae became my replacement. People know Paris Janae as the half-dressed, sexy R&B singer with sexual, raunchy lyrics, but the Paris Janae I knew was not like that at all. Yeah, she's selling records, touring, and doing numbers, but that wasn't the image she wanted. I remember when Paris Janae first got signed to the label. She was like a little sister to me, still in high school, very shy, had this good-girl, clean image, and wanted to sing gospel music, but that wasn't the plan the label had for Paris. When you're signed to certain labels, it comes with perks, but you don't get as much control as you think. Either you do what they say, look how they want you to look, sing the music they want you to sing, or get dropped without warning, possibly blackballed from the business, and get replaced by a singer who is almost ten years younger than you.

[Tiffani Blake:] What would you say are the pros and cons of being an independent artist now?

[Imani:] The pros are the freedom, control, and ownership I have over my music. The con is the financial responsibility that I have now.

[Tiffani Blake:] You're one of the best-dressed people in the game. You're always killing it. Your style is sexy and show-stopping, and you're a true fashionista.

[Imani:] I'm from Detroit, of course, I know how to dress, and it's in my blood. I got pictures of my daddy in the nineties wearing suits, Gators, and minks. My mama, who was his girl, stayed dressed to impress and was a mothafucking showstopper. My auntie was the same way; she kept her hair laid, wore badass boots and leather Pelle coats, and would pull her mink out in the winter. Detroit is the fashion and hair capital of the world.

[Tiffani Blake:] As beautiful as you are, you must get hit on a lot. Are you dating someone in the industry?

[Imani:] I'm dating someone, but that person is not in the industry.

[Tiffani Blake:] Rumors have been circulating about your sexuality. Do you like girls?

[Imani:] Do you like girls, Tiff?

[Tiffani Blake:] I'm the one who's supposed to be interviewing you. Don't be ashamed if you do.

[Imani:] First of all, I'm not ashamed of who I am; I like what I like; however, I'm a private person, and it's nobody's fucking business whether I like girls or guys. A well-known music producer started a rumor about my sexuality because he wanted to fuck me and didn't. However, the media should focus on my music and talent, not my sexuality.

[Tiffani Blake:] Let's revisit the past. You once said that your childhood was a mixture of good and bad memories. Talk about your childhood and upbringing.

[Imani:] A single mother raised me. My mama had four children. I grew up with two sisters and one brother. I don't have memories of my daddy because he died when I was very young. We were on welfare, but my mama also made money from doing hair. I didn't feel like a poor child because we were spoiled. We had toys, dolls, bikes, and nice clothes, and my little brother had a video game system. I lived on Euclid, off Fourteenth Street, near Linwood. I lived in the hood, but I felt like I lived in one of the best neighborhoods ever because everything was within walking distance: my schools, the recreation center, Duffield Library, playgrounds, the grocery store, Little Caesars Pizza, the Chinese food restaurant, and the beauty supply store. The beauty supply store was my favorite store because I would spend all my money on costume jewelry and makeup.

[Tiffani Blake:] What is one childhood memory that you'll never forget?

[Imani:] At the beginning of my career, I saved a lot of money doing my makeup for shows and interviews. I was in the choir at Thirkell Elementary School in the fourth grade. We had our spring concert, and I did my makeup for the performance. I snuck my makeup to school and did it in the girls' bathroom. I'm on stage wearing blue eye shadow, bright red lipstick, and mascara. I'm on stage singing, looking like a hot mess, but I thought I was cute. I can see my mama in the audience looking pissed. When we got home, she whupped my ass, told me that I was on stage looking like a little hooker, and told me to wash that shit off my face. I was in my room crying after my ass-whupping, and she called me into the bathroom. She wiped the tears off my face and started teaching me how to do makeup, and that's how I learned to do my makeup.

[Tiffani Blake:] And your makeup is always on fleek.

[Imani:] Thank you. I've always been a girly girl, but I knew how to fight. You had to know how to fight in my hood. My mama told me if I got my ass whupped in the streets, she would whup my ass. I'm a Cancer, and I've always been sensitive. I don't like being teased or talked about. I was my mama's problem child and was always getting into fights and getting in trouble in school. If you ask my sister or brother who my mama's baddest kid was, they'll say it was me. My siblings were getting good grades and on the honor roll, but I wasn't doing as well in school. I was going to Hutchins Middle School when the teachers wanted to put me in special education classes. It wasn't that I couldn't do the work; I wasn't dumb, I just didn't like school. My mind was elsewhere in class, and I was always either daydreaming or writing songs and poems in class. Plus, I had behavioral issues, and when the teachers got fed up with bad kids, the teachers recommended that the troubled kids be put in special classes. My great-aunt was mean to me as a child and would call me dumb, stupid, and retarded, because of my academic performance. That really fucked with my self-esteem.

[**Tiffani Blake:**] That's mean. Why were you acting out?

[**Imani:**] I had issues going on at home. I wasn't angry for no reason. I've experienced childhood trauma. I was molested, and then, on top of that, my little sister was killed in a drive-by shooting at six years old. It was on the news. She was outside playing with my little brother, and I was in the house when I heard the gunshots. My mama ran outside, and I will never forget the sounds of her screams. When I got outside, my mama was screaming with my little sister bleeding in my mama's arms. My little sister was my little best friend and partner in crime, and she didn't deserve to be killed. My little brother was so traumatized that he went to live with his daddy for the remainder of his childhood because my little sister got shot right in front of him, and he would wake up screaming from nightmares. I still have nightmares of what happened that day. To this day, I don't like the sound of guns; I don't like anything that sounds like a gun. I don't like firecrackers or any loud booming noises.

[**Tiffani Blake:**] Losing your little sister and being sexually abused as a child had to be difficult. Do you care to reveal the person who was sexually abusing you?

[Imani:] It was my mama's boyfriend at the time. He used to make me perform oral sex on him. The first time he made me do this was when I was twelve. He made money in the streets like my daddy, and he seemed like this cool guy at first. The first time I met him, my mama had introduced him to us, and he saw me crying. I was eleven at the time, and my great-aunt bought my siblings and kids from the neighborhood ice cream from the ice cream truck, but she didn't buy me shit. I started crying. He saw what happened to me and took me to Alma's Dairy Whip on Linwood, gave me a twenty-dollar bill, let me buy whatever, and I was able to keep the change. We thought my mama's boyfriend was cool because he gave us money, took us out, let us cuss, and never whupped us. He was more like a silly big brother than a dad. I remember when he let me wear his Cartier glasses to school. He used to tell me how pretty I was. I celebrated my birthday with my little brother every year. My little brother had just turned eight, and I had turned twelve. On my twelfth birthday, we went shoe shopping, played at Jeepers in Northland, went skating at Northland Roller Rink, and ate at TGI Fridays in Southfield. It seemed like the best birthday until that night.

[Tiffani Blake:] Did your mother know what was going on at the time?

[Imani:] No, I was scared to tell her, but I wish I had told her at that time. I didn't tell her until years later. My mama didn't play when it came to her kids. If my mama knew what was going on, she would be in prison for killing him. She didn't allow us to spend the night at too many people's houses, including the houses of family members. A lot of times, molestation happens within the family, but it's swept under the rug.

[Tiffani Blake:] Were your siblings sexually abused by the same man who abused you?

[**Imani:**] No, but I wasn't his only victim. He had gotten a fifteen-year-old pregnant and gave her abortion money. He never sexually penetrated me, not that it makes what he did to me less wrong. He and my mama used to fight a lot because she accused him of cheating. She knew something wasn't right, but she didn't know that he was cheating with minors.

[**Tiffani Blake:**] Where is he now?

[**Imani:**] He's dead. He was beefing with some niggas, and they were shooting at him when my little sister got killed. The night before the shooting happened, he tried to abuse me again sexually, but for some reason, my mama woke up in the middle of the night, saying that she couldn't sleep, and luckily, nothing happened that night. I remember going to bed, wishing that he was dead, and my wish came true the next day. Before I stopped going to church, the pastor talked so much about forgiveness. I will never forgive that mothafucka for what he did to me. If there's a heaven and a hell, I hope that he's burning in hell. I have a hard time trusting people because of what happened to me as a child. I trusted him, and he did the worst thing anyone had ever done to me. I didn't deserve to be molested; no one does. I'm sorry for crying.

[**Tiffani Blake:**] Don't you dare apologize for crying. It's okay to cry. Imani, you are so brave for telling your story.

[**Imani:**] I have no empathy for sexual abusers. Aside from what happened to me, I had a friend who was so pretty, and all the boys liked her. She was raped, but them niggas told the hood that she let them run a train on her. She wore short skirts, tight clothes, and makeup, and people thought she was fast, so they believed the rumor. Just like I was scared to say something, she was scared to say something. Her mama was on crack, and she told me that if she told what happened to her, they threatened to rape her again, kill her crackhead-ass mama, and rape her big sister. These stories need to be told. Sexual abuse is way too common. There are so many victims out there, especially in the music industry. They're just afraid to speak up. Some of your favorite music artists are rapists and pedophiles.

[Tiffani Blake:] The statistics are both staggering and disheartening. According to various studies, one in three women and one in six men experience some form of sexual violence in their lifetime. For those who have experienced sexual abuse, it is important to recognize that help is available. Numerous organizations and resources provide assistance, counseling, and advocacy for survivors. RAINN, known as Rape, Abuse & Incest National Network, is a prominent organization in the United States, offering a National Sexual Assault Hotline and online support through RAINN-dot-org. The number for the National Sexual Assault Hotline is one-eight-hundred, six-five-six, four-six-seven-three. Again, that number is one-eight-hundred, six-five-six, four-six-seven-three.

[Imani:] After I'm done exposing this industry, I don't care what happens to me.

After watching Imani's interview, I closed my laptop and broke down in tears. That was the first time I had heard Imani's story, and neither Imani nor Simone had ever told me it.

CHAPTER 20

Stolen Innocence

"Yeah, just like that. Keep sucking, don't stop," Dame said.

I was only twelve, performing oral sex on my mama's boyfriend. My mama, Elijah, and Aaliyah were asleep in the other rooms. Ayesha was at Kierra's house. This was the first time that it happened.

Earlier, Elijah yelled, "I wanna go to Jeepers!"

"I wanna go skating!" I yelled.

It was the day of my twelfth birthday, and I argued with Elijah about where we wanted to go.

"Y'all better figure out something, or we won't be going nowhere," Mama said.

"We already went to Jeepers for Leelee's birthday, Mama," I said.

"Pick a place, or we'll all be staying in the house today," Mama replied.

"Jeepers!"

"Skating!"

"Since you two can't agree, I'll let Leelee decide," Mama said. "Where you wanna go, Leelee? Jeepers or skating?" Mama asked Aaliyah.

"Jeepers!" Aaliyah replied.

"Jeepers, it is. Go get dressed," Mama told us.

"Mama, that's not fair," I whined.

"I'll tell you what. We can do both. We can go to Jeepers, and we'll go skating, and I'm taking y'all to Kids Foot Locker to get some new Jordans to rock," Dame said.

"Really?" I said in excitement.

"Yeah," Dame replied.

"You know how much money that is?" Mama said.

"Baby, that shit is car change to me. I got it," Dame said.

Elijah, Aaliyah, and I yelled, "Yay!"

"You are so good to my kids," Mama said as she kissed Dame.

It was Saturday, and our first stop was Northland Mall, where we went to Kids Foot Locker to buy shoes, and then Jeepers, where we played games and rode the rides. Our next stop was to Northland Roller Rink to skate, and we ended the night by eating at TGI Fridays.

I enjoyed being a kid. I still played with Barbies and Bratz dolls, watched cartoons, loved skating, and enjoyed riding the roller coaster at Jeepers. I wasn't trying to be fast like some of the other girls I knew. Sucking dick at twelve had never crossed my mind. I couldn't believe this was happening. I wanted to cry and scream. I wanted my mama to wake up and save me. My innocence was stolen from me that night.

"Imani, come here," Dame said.

It was in the middle of the night, and I was on my way to the bathroom when Dame called me into the living room. He was sitting in the dark on the sofa, smoking a blunt and drinking a bottle of liquor.

I walked into the living room and playfully said, "What up doe?"

"Did you have fun earlier?" Dame asked.

"I had so much fun. This was the best birthday ever!"

Dame smiled and said to me, "Don't tell Elijah or Aaliyah this. They might get jealous, but you're my favorite."

"I am?"

"Yeah. That's why I spent a lot of money on you for your birthday, but I need you to pay me back," Dame said.

"Pay you back? I ain't got no money."

"You don't have to have money to pay me back. Sit down," Dame said as he placed me on his lap.

That's when I started to feel uncomfortable. I felt weird and nervous when I sat on Dame's lap. His eyes were sleepy and bloodshot red. I smelled the weed and alcohol on his breath. I just wanted to pee and go back to bed.

"Take a sip. I won't tell Simone if you don't," Dame said as he handed me the bottle of liquor.

I said after tasting the liquor, "Ugh! That shit's nasty!"

"I'll mix it with pop for you next time. Do you got a boyfriend, Imani?"

"No."

"I don't see why these little niggas ain't chasing you, as pretty as you are. You gonna be a bad mothafucka when you grow up. Simone better watch out. You a virgin?"

"Um… yes," I replied nervously.

"Don't be scared, I don't bite. I take that back. I be biting on your mama. Your mama got some good-ass pussy. I be tearing that ass up; I know you be hearing us."

I got off his lap and said, "I gotta go back to bed."

He sat me back on his lap and replied, "You ain't gotta go nowhere just yet."

I felt so disgusted and uncomfortable. Dame stared into my eyes with a sinister smirk before pulling his dick out. Dame then grabbed my hand and placed it on his dick.

"Rub on it," Dame commanded.

Feeling afraid, I did what he told me.

"Just like that, keep going," he whispered.

He then made me get on my knees, gently pushed my head on his dick, and made me suck it. I wanted to throw up. I knew what he was doing to me was wrong.

"Yeah, just like that. Keep sucking, don't stop. Open your mouth wider. Speed it up."

I kept sucking until he pulled it out and came. He shot his semen on my thigh.

"That wasn't so bad. You give good head like your mama. If you use less teeth, you'll give better head than her. Keep this between us, and don't tell anybody. If you tell Simone, she won't believe you."

I immediately went into the bathroom, threw up, and brushed my teeth like five times. I looked into the mirror with tears running down my face, feeling ashamed.

Imani's story will unfold in Rated-M Wrote It's next book, *The Book of Imani*. Thank you for reading *The Book of Ayesha*.

www.ingramcontent.com/pod-product-compliance
Lightning Source LLC
Chambersburg PA
CBHW070103260626

47160CB00004B/1293